The Worlds We Think We Know

The Worlds We Think We Know

Dalia Rosenfeld

MILKWEED EDITIONS

Published 2017 by Milkweed Editions
Printed in the United States of America
Cover design by Mary Austin Speaker
Cover art: *Migration*: Copyright © Andrey Remnev 2009
Author photo by Efrat Vital
17 18 19 20 21 5 4 3 2 1
First Edition

Milkweed Editions, an independent nonprofit publisher, gratefully acknowledges sustaining support from the Jerome Foundation; the Lindquist & Vennum Foundation; the McKnight Foundation; the National Endowment for the Arts; the Target Foundation; and other generous contributions from foundations, corporations, and individuals. Also, this activity is made possible by the voters of Minnesota through a Minnesota State Arts Board Operating Support grant, thanks to a legislative appropriation from the arts and cultural heritage fund, and a grant from the Wells Fargo Foundation. For a full listing of Milkweed Editions supporters, please visit milkweed.org.

Library of Congress Cataloging-in-Publication Data

Names: Rosenfeld, Dalia, author.
Title: The worlds we think we know : stories / Dalia Rosenfeld.
Description: Minneapolis, Minnesota : Milkweed Editions, 2017.
Identifiers: LCCN 2016032464 | ISBN 9781571311269 (cloth : alk. paper)
Classification: LCC PS3618.O8348 A6 2017 | DDC 813/.6--dc23
LC record available at https://lccn.loc.gov/2016032464

Milkweed Editions is committed to ecological stewardship. We strive to align our book production practices with this principle, and to reduce the impact of our operations in the environment. We are a member of the Green Press Initiative, a nonprofit coalition of publishers, manufacturers, and authors working to protect the world's endangered forests and conserve natural resources. *The Worlds We Think We Know* was printed on acid-free 100% postconsumer-waste paper by Edwards Brothers Malloy.

For my parents

Contents

Swan Street | 3
The Worlds We Think We Know | 20
Flight | 37
A Foggy Day | 54
Thinking in Third Person | 60

The Other Air | 73
Amnon | 79
Daughters of Respectable Houses | 90
Contamination | 107
Invasions | 114

The Next Vilonsky | 131
Two Passions for Two People | 144
A Famine in the Land | 149
The Gown | 160
The Four Foods | 168

Liliana, Years Later | 177
Vignette of the North | 191
Floating on Water | 207
Bargabourg Remembers | 225
Naftali | 234

Acknowledgments | 255

The Worlds We Think We Know

Swan Street

Wherever Misha goes, I follow him. He doesn't know that he is being followed as he sets out each morning, a dirty tote bag slung across his shoulder for all his day's needs. Even if he turned around he probably could not fathom me standing there, an extension of his own shadow, shrugging my shoulders and offering him an apple or a cigarette from the bottom of my purse. I suspect it would distress him to see me at such close range, unannounced, just as it distresses him now when, without turning around, he feels me two inches behind him, breathing on his neck. That's when he starts second-guessing himself, like a peddler pushing a shopping cart in a supermarket, and heads for the nearest men's room to shut himself in.

He wanted to move to America to start a new life, though there was nothing wrong with our old one. Back home we had a garden, and neighbors who waved to us from open windows. We had asphalt streets and steel rails, fine wines and fast trains, and when those were not enough, we also had a small grove of trees in our backyard high enough to house a family of woodpeckers. The only thing our life lacked was a pretext to change it. But people are full of surprises. One morning Misha tripped over a freshly dug hole in the yard and declared he could no longer live in a country that revealed a permanent frost beneath the surface of its soil. I could not persuade him to stay.

I would like to say that as a result of following Misha, my legs grew stronger and my waist slimmer, that my view of the world expanded to let in more light during the day and more darkness at night. But this would not have been a realistic outcome. Misha was like an autumn leaf caught in a swirl of wind: even on the most temperate of days he had only to turn a corner to find himself back at his point of departure, where he could set his bag down again and spill out its contents, pleased that they had survived his short journey, his new pocket dictionary still sheathed in protective plastic.

*

The Swan Street Bed and Breakfast was a turn-of-the-century establishment fitted with twelve rooms and a dining area doubling as a smoking lounge. A steep, winding staircase led from the front door to a small carpeted foyer, where guests could leave their suitcases while their beds were being made and admire a cheap reproduction of a Schaffhausen grandfather clock standing against the wall, its pendulum swinging back and forth like the trunk of a tired elephant.

From the moment Misha stepped in the door, I knew it would be hard to get him out again. Something about this place slowed him down, leadened his limbs to the point where he became, like the grandfather clock, a stationary fixture against the wall. The small store of energy he retained was at its most concentrated during breakfast, served every morning between seven and nine o'clock, the two hours that Misha used to dream his best dreams before crawling out of bed and putting on a pair of socks. Here, on Swan Street, he walked into the dining room at 6:30 a.m., showered and shaved, to sit with the manager while he emptied ashtrays into a cracked dustpan and arranged slices of cantaloupe on paper plates. At such an hour I was still sleeping, but my dreams had never been a source of much comfort to me, filled as they often were with smells and sounds rather than with visions.

The inertia typically set in after breakfast, when Misha had scheduled most of his appointments. Today his first is with Carlos, a Realtor in the south end of the city, where laundry hangs limply outside apartment windows and where Misha clumsily drops his dictionary down the shaft of an open manhole.

This is how I see him: On his way to Carlos's office, Misha stops to watch a street musician perform a Bach fugue on a synthesizer. He is not interested in the music, only in the fingers that create it, racing across the keys as if trying to keep pace with the pedestrians hurrying by. At the end of the performance he tosses a dollar into the musician's hat and recalls a time from his childhood when, upon spotting a foreigner, he and his friends would crowd around and ask to trade a coin from his country for one from their own. More often than not the foreigner would oblige, and the exchange would pass smoothly. But sometimes, after offering the boys a coin from his pocket, the man would continue on his way without accepting one in return, and Misha and his friends would throw it indignantly back at him, incensed at being taken for beggars.

A block away from his appointment, Misha stops at a phone booth and dials the real estate agency. "Hello, Carlos? It is Misha, from Swan Street," he announces. "I am afraid I cannot meet with you today. It seems I have misplaced something very dear to me and must try to retrieve it before it is too late. I am sorry for the inconvenience." Hanging up the phone, he glances at his watch; then he returns to the spot where he has lost his dictionary, and for five minutes stands over the manhole like a mourner at a grave site.

I do not scold Misha for missing his appointment. Instead I write him a note reminding him to contact Dr. Gutman as soon as possible to inquire about employment possibilities for the fall. Without Dr. Gutman's assistance, Misha would probably still be digging holes in our garden back home, searching for dry land. I do not know how to feel about that, or about the message he leaves with Dr. Gutman's secretary when he finally does call, backing out of the very project he had proposed only a month before. The next day Misha comes down with the flu, a bad case requiring a cold compress of raw potatoes and beets. When Dr. Gutman returns his call, it is all Misha can do not to retch into the receiver.

Walter, the proprietor on Swan Street, brings Misha hot tea and invites him to watch as he prepares to dye his beard from gray to red. "This is how I get my women," he explains, removing a small bottle of liquid from a paper bag and setting it down on the nightstand next to Misha. "Not with ice, but with fire."

In his feverish state, Misha feels me mop his brow with a damp cloth. "I got my woman also with fire," he says. "We were watching arcs of volcanic islands form in midocean on television. I have never seen so much lava and ash on a single channel."

Misha closes his eyes and falls asleep. I would not be so hard on him about finding an apartment if he were dreaming about me, or even about the volcano that lit the flame for our first kiss, ten years before. But it is Swan Street that ignites his imagination, leading him back even further in time, twenty years or more, when his one goal in life was to have enough hair on his chin to be able to look in the mirror and say, *There is no other man in this mirror but me.* In his dream, Walter stands at the sink, his full red beard sending streams of brown water spiraling down the drain. "I used to provide disposable razors for my guests," he says in a muffled tone. "But you don't look like you need one."

When Misha wakes up, Walter is washing his hands. "I've still got a stock of shower caps in the closet for the ladies, but they never ask for them anymore," Misha hears him say. "My wife wore a shower cap in the shower, a hairnet to work, and curlers to bed. In the three years that we were married, I never saw her completely naked."

Misha stares uncomprehendingly at Walter's back, dizzy from the chemical fumes rising out of the drain. For a moment his head fills with numbers and when he looks up at the mirror, he sees not two faces, but twenty, all lined up like ducks at a shooting gallery. "With your red hair, the women will think that you are from

Ireland, and that I am from America," he says, eliminating one face at a time with a carefully aimed blink. "That is the beauty of this country."

In my own quest for beauty I persuaded Misha, a few days before the flight to New York, to take a short trip to the coast, where we spent an afternoon walking along the water and discussing our plans for the future. As the sun began to set, Misha's attention shifted inland, to the crowds of people populating the beach, many calling it a day and packing up their umbrellas and empty picnic baskets to take back home.

Something about the sight of so many people leaving disturbed him, and when I expressed an interest in heading back myself, he sat down in the sand and refused to budge.

"For three or four hours we stare at the sea, and the water delights us," he reflected. "We spread out blankets that have never felt softer, eat hastily prepared sandwiches that have never tasted better, and soak up the sun like flowers in an open field. Then, at a certain moment between the third and fourth hours, the blanket starts to feel scratchy and we shake it out and roll it up. The picnic baskets that have provided our sustenance for the day lie overturned in the sand, and our stomachs crave a steaming bowl of soup, straight from the stove. Before closing our umbrellas we take one last look at the water and smile at the sun still reflected on its surface. But if we were asked to stay an hour longer, the mere sight of a seashell would make us sick, and at home we would fall asleep and dream that the sea was nothing but a big bathtub of dirty water."

Fortunately, Misha did not ask me to stay longer. As if roused from a nap by a cold wind, he rubbed his arms and looked blankly at the sky. "Let's go," he said simply, rising to his knees. Trailing him by a few feet all the way back to the car, I felt for the first time what it would be like to follow him, and it was a miserable feeling. There he was, my husband, almost within arm's reach, and yet as distant as the water we were leaving behind. His thoughts, his fears, the hopes that clung to him like the sand on his feet—I could not grab hold of any of them. It was like trying to enter someone else's dream and being turned away at the door. Reaching out to take Misha's arm, I closed the space between us and vowed never to follow him in that way again.

"The beauty of this country," Walter repeats, still rinsing his hands at the sink, "has just moved into room 10, right above yours. An architect. Maybe you'll get lucky, and she'll drop in to say hello."

Misha lifts his eyes up to the ceiling; a single crack, short and slightly curved, like a wrinkle in a brow, meets his glance. "Thank you for the information," he says. "I will brace myself for the fall."

The next morning he enters the dining room to find the woman from room 10 sitting at the table, reading a book.

"Good morning," Misha says, surprised she is alone. "I hear you are living above me."

The woman looks up from her book, marking her place with a piece of torn napkin. "And do you hear me living above you?"

"Not at all."

"That is the hallmark of a well-built house."

Eileen stays at the hotel for seven nights, a long time by most standards but regrettably short for Misha, who likens the color of her eyes to that of the frond of a fern and the slenderness of her neck to the tendril of a Peruvian lily. For the first three nights Misha falls asleep staring at the ceiling. On the fourth night Eileen knocks on the door with a signed copy of the book she has come to the city to promote, a three-hundred-page critique of an early proposal for the construction of St. Paul's Cathedral. It is she who finally persuades Misha to meet with a Realtor.

"You need to live in a building with a solid foundation, like an old flax-spinning mill, or a high-rise with a helicopter landing pad on the roof," she advises him on the sixth morning, as they walk through three empty rooms of a house flanked by vinyl siding. "You need ceilings that can't be reached with a stepladder."

Misha walks into the bathroom and runs his finger along the edge of the sink. "Yes, you are right," he agrees. "A low ceiling is like having someone reading over your shoulder twenty-four hours a day. No matter how hard you try to ignore him, you always see him out of the corner of your eye, waiting for you to turn the page. This is not the way I want to live in America."

It was my presence, of course, that Misha was trying to ignore, my profile that obstructed his view of Eileen, turning her luminous face into a haze of incongruous parts. I'd had no intention of accompanying my husband on this particular outing; it was enough that his voice was always buzzing in my ear, singing the praises of Swan Street. But before I could change my course, there I was, hot on his trail, sniffing furiously like a bloodhound in pursuit of its own master. That it was Misha himself who was holding the leash only made his footsteps harder to rub out.

The real estate agent waits outside the bathroom for her client to finish his conversation. "The owner is thinking about installing a hot tub," she says from the hallway. "Should I tell him you two would be interested?"

Misha peeks his head out the open door. "Thank you, I think we have seen enough," he says, speaking only for himself. "My wife will join me soon, and I do not want to show her America from a basin of boiling water."

*

The grandfather clock in the foyer has stopped working, but Misha does not notice. He has spent the morning at a used furniture store, looking for something that will give him more space for his underwear and socks and allow him to return the Bible to the nightstand drawer. In the past, Misha had all the space he wanted and always complained that it was not enough. But in America, in a room in which he can barely move, he breathes in the air around him like a claustrophobe coming out of a closet. He is quick to forget that smoking has left him with weak lungs.

When the saleswoman approaches, Misha becomes acutely aware of his accent. "Yes," "Thank you," "Over there," "Too large," he stutters, responding to her inquiries in as few words as possible. He observes the woman studying him and follows the trajectory of her eyes as they try to determine the provenance of his shoes, pants, shirt. *I live on Swan Street,* he reminds himself, *named after the constellation Cygnus, a cluster of stars far beyond the reaches of our galaxy.* Clearing his throat, he mutters a few more words and wonders in which direction his accent will take her next—to the overpriced dresser in the corner, its tapered legs cut from seasoned mahogany, or to the cheap chest of drawers nearby. Unwilling to find out, he declines additional assistance and settles for a bookcase in the back room, whose widely spaced boards he estimates can hold a week's worth of laundry.

Back on Swan Street, Walter meets him in the foyer, shaking his head. "If the mainspring goes, the pendulum goes with it," he says, pointing to the empty space behind him. "That clock was like a second heart to me."

Misha looks at the indentation in the carpet where the grandfather clock used to stand. "The clock is gone? I will miss it."

Continuing down the hallway, he hugs the bookcase close to his chest. Walter follows. "That looks like it would make a pretty piece of firewood," he says, banging one of the boards with his fist.

"I think I will put it against the wall, next to my night table." Misha unlocks his door and sets the shelf down in front of it. "That would give me enough room to still climb out of bed in the morning and not stub my toe."

When Misha and I moved into our first apartment together, he wanted to keep it sparse. We furnished the rooms with only the bare necessities and dwelled in our new home like peasants living off the land. One day I came home with a shoe rack to mount behind the bedroom door and Misha, disapproving, told me about a Bulgarian perfume expressed from rose petals that used two hundred pounds of blossoms to make a single ounce of oil. "If twenty pairs of shoes suspended in the air would help bring out the essence of a woman's foot, you would be the talk of Europe," he said cynically.

Walter bangs again at the bookshelf, then wags a tobacco-stained finger under Misha's nose. "Anyone who is afraid of stubbing his toe shouldn't make himself too comfortable," he says, stepping deeper into the room. "If you ask me, we've already got too many toes on our feet to begin with."

Misha is sitting in bed writing a letter to me when Eileen knocks on the door. "I've come to say good-bye," she says, and cups her hand like a fortune-teller around the brass dome of the bedpost.

Misha puts away the letter and swings his legs around to the edge of the bed. "I'm sorry you're leaving." He looks at the clock next to him but does not register the time. "I was hoping you could accompany me to a few more apartments before you left."

"Well, it just so happens—" Eileen pauses to remove a single key from her breast pocket.

"Yes?"

"—that I've got one left to show you."

It was into the body of another woman, the ultimate dwelling place, that Misha was led that night. Eileen left him little choice: she was beautiful; she was radiant; she was America. But Swan Street was equally responsible, having conspired to turn a mathematician, with a mind always on the move, into a body at rest. After a month Misha had already forgotten how wide his range of reflexes used to be, and when Eileen steered him into uncharted territory, he could not distinguish the mountains from the trees and fell into her arms like a bird shot by a poison arrow, limp, dazed, and defenseless.

How many caresses did it take before he sprang back to life? How much flesh had to unveil itself for my husband to surrender to its softness?

Back home Misha would have been in better control. In a country so vast it takes almost half a day for the sun's rays to cross it, he would have found the means to fend off Eileen's advances—a slight tightening of the lips, an elaborate rotation of the hands, a quick succession of words, in his own tongue, that establishes a boundary between man and woman as between two countries separated by a broad river. Gently but categorically he would have made his resistance clear and kept the door open, allowing Eileen to leave shamed but with her dignity still intact, a leopardess cowed by the sight of her own spots. But in the end it was Misha who suffered the humiliation of it all, when Walter visited Eileen's room the next morning with her breakfast and found him sprawled out on the bed, snoring like an old asthmatic. "No overnight guests," he warned the two lovers. "Screwing anyone other than your spouse puts a strain on the box springs, and those bastards are over fifty years old."

Misha finishes the letter he writes, but sends others instead. For the next few days I am still with him, urging him to get out into the world and become a part of it. Misha listens and adds his voice to my own; his ears ring like a bell cracked down the middle.

When the first of his letters finally does arrive, I am sitting in the garden, fanning myself with the day's newspaper. The mailman sees me and deviates a few steps from his route, handing me Misha's letter without giving it a glance.

I stare at the stamps on the letter, two American flags fluttering in the wind. I want this to be the last one, the final page in the biography of a man whose story should have belonged to someone else. I want to remember what our life was like before letters, when Swan Street was as far away as the galaxy after which it was named, and Misha and I slept side by side in a bed shaped by only our bodies. I think it nothing short of shameless when, the next day, the mailman brings me another letter, and then another. Now that there is nothing left to say, Misha has discovered a second tongue at the tip of his pen, and he slobbers over the paper like a baby learning to speak.

*

One morning Dr. Gutman called and invited Misha to the institute to take a look at his prospective office. "I need a landsman for the project," he insisted, once more offering Misha the job he had rejected a month before. "The American I hired in your place tried to turn everything upside down."

As he stretched his legs out on the bed, Misha could

feel what it would be like to get up and go. From three miles away he could see Dr. Gutman sit him down at a cubicle the size of an outhouse and say, "This is your chair, this is your desk, these are your colleagues. Make yourself at home."

It would have been the wrong thing to say. Misha was a runaway, and home the hot breath on his neck he tried to shake off as he ran.

"If I could take some work back to the hotel with me, I could start immediately," Misha replied quickly, winding the telephone cord around his wrist to keep himself rooted in place. "I'm still looking for an apartment."

"There's a sofa in my office that opens up to a bed. It's yours for the asking."

"Thank you for the offer. I'll think it over."

Five minutes later Misha is sipping tea from a Styrofoam cup in the Swan Street lounge.

Walter walks in from the kitchen, holding up a wet and wrinkled tea bag. "Is this yours?" he asks.

Misha nods. "I thought I might have a second cup. Will you join me?"

"In America we use something once and throw it away. That's the rule."

"I am glad you do not feel this way about your guests." Misha loosens his nervous grip on the cup, for fear of crushing it.

"Oh, but I do. My guests are as disposable as everything in this kitchen," Walter says. "When one has used himself up, another will soon be standing in the hallway, waiting for his key. I haven't had a vacant room for more than three days since I opened up the place."

After his tea, Misha goes back to his room to lie down. He has lost weight since coming to America and cannot burrow into the mattress as he used to. His body stays fixed to the surface, light and motionless as the air around him. Closing his eyes, he listens to the sounds of footsteps on the other side of his door. More guests have arrived, and he is glad.

The sounds outside fade and are gradually replaced by Misha's own breathing. His lungs slowly fill with air traveling upward all the way to the tip of his tongue, which rests against his lips as though in preparation to speak. This is how he used to go to sleep when he was at his most content, words forming in his mouth and then falling away again, like a group of children met by a closed park gate. Sometimes I would make my own voice express what Misha could not, and tell him that I loved him. His lips would twitch a little, then close tighter than before. He never stayed awake long enough to respond.

Walter is setting the table for breakfast the next morning when Misha enters the dining room and hands him his credit card.

"For another good night's sleep, and for my first dream in English. I do not remember any of it, only that everything I said came out in a whisper, and nobody knew whether I was speaking to them or to myself."

Walter tosses the credit card onto the table. "The room needs to be vacated by tomorrow," he says matter-of-factly. "If you're lucky, it won't rain until the day after."

Misha remains seated. "Vacated? But my room needs no such thing."

"The room needs what I need."

"I see," says Misha. He marvels at how quickly Walter's red beard has returned to gray.

On the wall hangs a mirror ornamented with arabesques and winged horses. Misha stares at the horses, half expecting them to take flight, and then at himself next to them. "Perhaps you need a new face for the room, some new blood to circulate through the veins of the house. Yes?"

"Mm."

"But you should know that my blood has just arrived to this country. It is just off the boat, as you say."

Walter stares out the window, blinking at the sun as it signals the start of day. "You can leave the bookcase in the foyer if you're not taking it with you. I'm expecting a group of tourists from Japan in a few weeks. They might need a place to put their cameras."

"Thank you. I will take the bookcase with me."

Wrapping a blueberry muffin in a napkin, Misha returns to his room to finish the last letter I will receive from Swan Street, or from any other street in this new country he has come to call home.

I waited one season for my husband to return. I stood for hours in the hot summer sun, hoping for ice to appear in the subsoil and for Misha to suddenly spring up behind me and shout, "You see! You see!" When it was time to put in the storm windows, I began to give up hope. The screws came loose after the first heavy rain, and the glass rattled every time the wind blew.

Lying in bed at night, I think of Misha as he continues his weary journey on foot, traversing deep jungles and remote tundra every time he crosses the street. Today our garden is a blur of buttercups too bright to be picked. I shudder at the thought that one day a cold wind will come to America and catch my husband by surprise. I suspect that he is waiting for it even now, in his sandals and short sleeves, and that it is only a matter of time before it fills him with the force of its current and blows him, in one icy breath, where he wants to go.

THE WORLDS WE THINK WE KNOW

The onions Lotzi ate could be smelled five floors below him in the lobby of Migdal Zahav, the Golden Tower Retirement Home in Jerusalem, where he lived. Lotzi always waited for me to arrive before retrieving his knife from the cupboard, a gesture that was never lost on me since I feared he would one day use it to take his life. With one clean cut the onion would separate into two halves, each half rocking on its domed back for a second or two before coming to rest on the countertop. Lotzi ate it with bread, one slice for every three bites of onion, and washed it down with a cup of tepid Wissotzky made from old teabags reduced to the size of walnuts. He always offered me tea but never anything to eat, as though the onion and bread were part of a ritual reserved for him alone, a Jew from Lvov who had lost everything but the taste for bitterness and dry bread.

I never asked him any questions, and he never gave me any answers. We each knew where the other came from, and that seemed to be enough. When my training session at AMCHA had ended and the group leader handed out our assignments, she reminded each volunteer to make contact as soon as possible. "Many survivors who wake up in the morning do not know whether living another day is a blessing or a curse," she said by way of parting. "You will make it a blessing for them."

Every week I sat across from Lotzi at his small kitchen table and waited for his story to begin. Not everyone was so hesitant to talk; just the other day, standing in line at the *shuk* for tomatoes, I was grabbed at the wrist by a childhood friend of Anne Frank's and made to understand that Anne would have grown up to look just like me. Lotzi sat with his onion and bread and tea and said nothing. Occasionally he would raise his head and clear his throat, and I would tell myself to get ready, to brace myself for what was to come. Then he would hack into a napkin and continue eating.

*

One morning from my bedroom window on Jabotinsky Street, I saw a young man and woman dressed in overalls digging up pansies from the square that separates the president's residence from the prime minister's. I went downstairs for a closer look; the flowers were disappearing quickly, and from the roots. After a bus went by I crossed the street and stood in front of the pair, staring at the garbage bag filling up by their feet. The man looked up first, then the woman. "What do you want?" they both said at the same time. I shrugged and asked, "Are you planning to sell those?" The woman struck her spade into the earth, working the roots like a kibbutznik. "Not to you," she said.

For a full three weeks I stopped visiting Lotzi, thinking I had better things to do. I bought a bicycle and rode it, first only up and down Jabotinsky, then branching out onto busier streets where I often found myself stuck behind a taxi or a tour bus waiting for the light to turn green. I didn't like the bicycle much and made it a point never to lock it. By the beginning of the third week the city had become a blur, and I abandoned the bike next to a pretzel cart outside Jaffa Gate. When I returned to Lotzi he looked at me blankly, as though he had never seen me before, or perhaps as though I had never been gone. We sat at his kitchen table in silence, and he ate his onion and bread. I didn't apologize for my absence. Before I left, he lifted his head and said, "Cars in America are big, eh?" There was nothing cryptic in his words; it was just a simple question asked by a simple man. Still, I spent the rest of the day wondering what it meant. It was the only question Lotzi ever asked me.

The first young person I spent time with in Jerusalem was Srulik. It was not by choice that this happened, but because of the reserved seating imposed on each holder of a Cinematheque pass. At every screening, Srulik and I sat one row apart, his mop of red curls clashing with the upholstery of the seats until the lights were dimmed and his fire snuffed out. Sometimes he arrived late and the space in front of me would suddenly darken, like one shadow eclipsing another. At the end of the screening, before the lights even came back on, Srulik would swiftly turn around to ask whether I had enjoyed the movie. From the expression on my face, which always registered displeasure, he must have thought I hated them all.

We had coffee together only once, upstairs at the Cinematheque cafe, overlooking the Old City. I learned everything I cared to learn about Srulik in those forty-five minutes. He was trained as a lawyer but had never worked as one. He had been a tour guide in the army. He was from a kibbutz in the Negev that supplied the entire country with chocolate pudding. About me, Srulik wanted to know more than I was willing to share. Twice during the course of our conversation he said enigmatically, in response to information I gave, "I know; I can tell." When I did not ask him to elaborate, the eagerness in his face faded and he excused himself to go to the bathroom. Srulik moved ponderously; he had huge feet and a body that in its bulkiness seemed not to want to follow their lead. I felt sorry for him but for myself as well. When Srulik returned, I looked at him with great intensity and asked myself whether I might feel just a little less sorry for myself if I slept with him a single time. From across the table I could smell the medicinal scent of bathroom soap on his hands. More sorry, I decided, not less.

*

One afternoon I knocked on Lotzi's door and nobody answered. I had arrived a few minutes late but no later than usual, and I was not ready to consider the possibility that these few minutes which I'd spent brushing my teeth or looking for my shoes or stopping at the Jerusalem Theater to check a showtime were significant enough to be registered by anything but a clock. I put my ear to the door and knocked again; this time it opened. Inside stood a young man in an army uniform, a pair of thick black eyebrows fringing his face like epaulets. I took one look at him and had to muffle the sound of my breathing, as though I had been running for days and had only just found a reason to slow down. He moved aside to let me in, and I saw Lotzi at his usual place at the table, his eyes fixed on some faraway spot.

I spoke to Lotzi more that day than in all my other visits combined. I told him about my life in New Jersey, the strip malls and the synagogues, and about my parents, who had raised me to be the kind of Jew who could plant a tree in Israel without having to stay and watch it grow. I told him about my fondness for movies, and about another survivor I visited who always spun a globe while she spoke. I told him I liked falafel. The young man who was not Lotzi listened politely to my ramblings but did not respond. Lotzi did the same. When I was through, I stood up and asked Lotzi for a glass of water. "Help yourself," he said agreeably, and continued eating.

At the sink, I waited for some movement in the room that did not originate from me. A few nights before at the Cinematheque I had watched Srulik plop himself down in a seat at the opposite end of the theater, in defiance of the rules, and felt a momentary pang of guilt at the thought that I was causing him to suffer. Then a young woman sat down next to him, a braid like challah winding down her back, and pecked him on the cheek just as the lights were starting to dim. With a twinge of regret, I realized that I had probably not caused him to suffer enough.

The sound of running water seemed to rouse Lotzi, who turned to me attentively. "In Lvov there was no falafel," he said while I drank. "In Lvov there was Jewish food."

On any other day I would have reacted to this statement like a mother to her baby's first words, but as Lotzi spoke, the soldier was slinging his backpack across his shoulder and heading for the door. "I'm off," he said, but did not open it. Outside it had started to rain, obstructing the view from the living room window, and I knew that if I did not permit myself a good look before he left I would not have a chance to do so afterward, from five stories above. "Where are you going?" I blurted out. "It's raining. Do you have an umbrella?" The soldier turned to me with surprise. "I have a car," he replied casually. "Do you want a ride?"

We drove across the city to his apartment. It was rush hour and the cars were relentless, linked to one another like the segmented tail of some ugly animal. As we inched along, I allowed myself to study Yair's face, the lines that converged around the corners of his eyes, the thick vein that bulged from his neck whenever he honked the horn. He noticed my gaze. "What are you looking at?" he asked shyly, his mouth sprouting new lines, curved like the crest of a wave. "A map of Israel," I said, smiling back.

When we arrived at his flat, Yair tossed his backpack on the couch and made straight for the fridge. "Are you hungry?" he asked, concealing himself within the cold rectangular box. "Yes," I said. A few minutes later we were eating by candlelight, an array of cheeses, pickled salads, stuffed vegetables, and pita spread out before us on the kitchen table. I waited for the food to fill me with the courage to speak, then said, "So how do you know Lotzi?" Before answering, Yair poured himself a glass of wine and drank half of it. "I don't," he said.

That night I saw Yair without his army uniform. A *hamsin* had blown in from the desert, filling the air with a fine sand and stray refuse from the Jerusalem streets: candy wrappers, plastic bags, pages of newspaper swirling as though in search of a fish to wrap themselves around. Yair's uniform looked cleaner than the shirt I had been wearing all day, a white tank top quickly going gray. Sitting on his bed, he handed me each article of clothing as it came off: socks, pants, shirt, undershirt, boxers. I held the bundle close and waited for my body to absorb its earthy smell. Then I tossed it onto the floor and let my own clothes fall on top.

Afterward Yair told me he had to leave the next morning, and that while he was away communicating would be difficult. "Nobody likes guarding checkpoints," he said, turning on his side and leaning into his palm. "But the snipers are willing to wait all day for that one soldier stupid enough to try to make a phone call while on duty."

In New Jersey I had once told a man I thought I loved that I wanted to go with him wherever he went. "Even to Trenton?" he had asked, smiling. I looked at Yair, his body taking up the length of the bed, and tried to imagine the people who wished to do him harm seeing him like this, naked, the curve of his clavicle resembling the curve of their clavicles, the absence of foreskin on his penis resembling their own penises. "Doesn't your mother go out of her mind?" I asked.

"My mother passed away a few years ago," Yair said. "But yes, she would have."

"And your father?"

"My father is a patient man."

*

In the morning Yair filled a bowl with cucumbers and tomatoes, and we ate breakfast on his balcony overlooking the Shufersal and a slight suggestion of the Judean Hills behind it. He was in uniform again; in the middle of the night I had woken from a dream and decided to wash it. Before Yair hugged me good-bye, I asked him whether wearing a clean uniform made it more or less likely that he would be the target of an attack. Throughout breakfast I had played a paranoid's game of Russian roulette, stabbing the vegetables in my salad and counting what came onto the fork before I ate it: more cucumbers than tomatoes meant there was nothing to worry about and Yair would be safe; more tomatoes than cucumbers, and our happiness would be cut short. Yair led me inside and sat me down on the bed, and I watched him put on the same pair of boots I had seen him take off the night before. "If my mother were alive, she would have asked the very same question," he said, leaning over to kiss me on the cheek. "And I would have answered her the same way I'm going to answer you."

"How?"

He kissed me on the cheek again.

*

After Yair left, an early spring virus swept through Jerusalem, creating a panic among the old German Jews of Rehavia, where I lived. Jabotinsky Street was teeming with Filipina live-ins sent out by their elderly charges to stock up on boxes of tissues and bottled water. They walked alone, wheeling collapsible metal carts behind them, the look of agreeability on their faces contrasting sharply with the cross-grained impatience of the Israelis who raced past them. My neighbor Mrs. Spangenthal, who had fired her Filipina for repeatedly failing to remove the bones from her fish, sought my help after returning from the *makolet* on the corner with more than she could carry. Together we carried three cases of Evian up two flights of stairs, Mrs. Spangenthal pausing at the landing to catch her breath and count the years that had passed since her husband's heart had given out. "Did I tell you my husband died?" she said to me before we parted, her eyes brimming over. "Ten years now."

Every day I waited for Yair to call, and every day he called, sometimes in the middle of the night when the city was so quiet I felt I could not raise my voice above a whisper, and sometimes first thing in the morning to the sounds of the muezzin floating from the Old City through my open window. I told Yair that I missed him and that everyone in Jerusalem was at home, sick in bed. He asked after my own health, shouting into the receiver as though the subject caused him great concern. Through the static I tried to identify the noises in the background, hoping to hear something to make me worry less about where he was: a snatch of conversation, a toilet flushing, the wheels of a car being let through and driving harmlessly by. Before we hung up Yair asked when I was planning to visit Lotzi again, and for a split second I didn't know whom he was talking about. Then I said, "Today. Right now, in fact," and glanced out the window to see if it was raining.

From my apartment the way to Migdal Zahav was all downhill, past schools and post offices, Ottoman-era houses and cinder block structures hiding behind coils of bougainvillea, and street signs chronicling the country's history, much of which I discovered I still needed to learn. As I approached Lotzi's building a rush of diesel fumes from a Tnuva milk truck assailed me, and I coughed all the way to the fifth floor. Outside Lotzi's door I heard more coughing, like the cracking of dry branches, and I wondered if the fumes could have followed me that far. Then I remembered the virus.

Lotzi opened the door just wide enough to tell me to come back tomorrow. "In the morning," he managed in a single breath. "*Ba'boker.*"

I waited for the door to fly open and Yair to pull me over the threshold. "Do you need anything, Lotzi?" I asked through the crack. "Do you have enough food? Are you drinking?"

"*Ba'boker,*" he repeated.

At the end of the hallway, an old woman emerged from her apartment, holding on to a walker for support. "Why all the shouting?" she wanted to know, taking tentative steps toward me. I let her come a little closer. "Lotzi is sick." I pointed to the door, which was begging to be pushed open, and tried not to think about who would nurse Lotzi back to health if not me. "And who isn't?" the woman retorted. She stopped in her tracks, as if waiting for an answer, then turned around and shuffled back to her room.

"I'll come tomorrow morning," I promised Lotzi through the crack. "*Ba'boker.*" He didn't answer, but I knew he had heard me. The sound of his coughing accompanied me all the way down the corridor.

On the way home I saw a group of German tourists gathered around the square with the flower bed that had been denuded a few weeks before. A young Israeli tour guide stood listlessly at the helm, shielding her face from the sun with her hand, and directed everyone's attention to the new plantings. "Here are some pretty flowers indigenous to Jerusalem," she said of the common pansies clustered at her feet. "Around the corner at the president's residence, you will see more." One of the tourists glanced at the flowers, then reached down to run his fingers along the perforated black tube lying under them. "Is this strange snake the source of their hydration?" he asked doubtfully, removing a handkerchief from his pocket. The tour guide looked down and readjusted the rubber with the toe of her shoe. "Yes, it is," she said. "It's a slow-release system and one of

Israel's greatest agricultural achievements. You will see more of them at the president's residence."

When Yair called in the evening, I was all worked up. In my mind's eye I could still see the German tourists standing in a semicircle around the network of tubes and flowers, shaking their heads in schadenfreude at the ugliness of the whole enterprise, at the failure of the Jewish state to meet even the minimum standard of aesthetics and self-respect. Forgetting for a moment where he was, I asked Yair what he thought about the black irrigation snakes swallowing up the flowers they were meant to sustain. "Why can't they be buried under the soil with the beetles and worms?" I wanted to know. "Why do they have to be so conspicuous?"

"I don't even notice them," Yair said.

"But the Germans do."

"I don't notice the Germans either."

We spoke for as long as circumstances would allow, the cord of the telephone wrapped around my finger like a resistant lock of hair. I wanted Yair to understand that he had existed in my imagination for years, that he had been part of the landscape I longed for but could never find, as real as the Jerusalem stone and the driftwood from the wadis that surrounded me now. But how could I explain it? I told him that in Israel when the sun blazed I did not suffer from the heat, and that when it rained I did not run to seek shelter. He laughed at the melodrama in my voice and said he understood, that I didn't need to try to explain anything at all. "And when will I see you again?" he asked when our time had run out.

I filled my lungs with the sound of Yair's voice and swallowed. "That's what I should be asking you."

"So ask."

"Ask? But I'm seeing you now."

*

In the morning, when the Muslims of the Old City were summoned to their mosques and Christians rose to the reverberations of church bells one quarter over, I waited for something to call me, to coax me like a snake charmer from the coil of my sleep and lift me to a higher state of being. There were plenty of Jewish sounds around me, but none was the sound I needed, the supplication of a stooped old man rapping at my window in search of a tenth soul for his minyan. This was the tradition of my shtetl ancestors, set against the squall of roosters and ruffians on horseback. During hard times, a wizened knuckle testing its strength against a drawn shutter was as loud as we could afford to be. For generations, it managed to make itself heard.

I remembered my promise to visit Lotzi.

A taxi was waiting in front of Migdal Zahav when I arrived. It was a Mercedes, a gift to Israel from a Germany still trying to make good. First I smelled the fumes from its snorting engine, and then I spotted Lotzi, leaning against the vehicle as if trying to check its pulse. I was surprised to see him there, a man too sick even for his own bed. But it was clear from the curve of his lip that he had some mission to accomplish and that nobody was going to stop him.

"Shalom, Lotzi, where are you going?" I waited for some sign that he was not sick anymore, a rush of color reaching his cheeks, a glint of recognition in his eye. It didn't occur to me that I had never seen him look any other way than he did now.

The driver was getting impatient; his cigarette had only a few sucks left. "Where are you going, Lotzi?" I repeated. This time he regarded me, and nodded his head slowly. "Come," he said, fumbling with the cab door. "There is still time if we hurry."

I climbed in.

Out the window, all of Jerusalem lay before me, but with Lotzi next to me the only landscape I could absorb was the thick veins in his neck, throbbing with agitation and old age. From his profile I could see that he had not shaved in days; his cheeks were sunken, as though struggling to support the excess stubble on them, and a scab had formed on his chin from some previous mishap. The driver charged through the city at a reckless pace, paying no heed to potholes or pedestrians or to his sick passenger in back, whose frail body was pulled every which way by the twists and turns of the taxi. When we came to an intersection, I noticed the rows of residential units giving way to tall hills and a sky bluer than before. "*L'an?*" I called out to the driver. *Where to?* "Kiryat Hayovel," he shouted without turning around. "Ask the old man."

The light turned green, and I saw exactly where we were. Yair's apartment building loomed before us, a gray slab of cement erupting from the ground like a weed in a garden. I stared at this eyesore with a pounding heart, not knowing if I was looking at a Jerusalem rebuilt or destroyed. On the balconies I could already see the heads of plants turning inward.

The taxi came to a halt at the entrance, and the music from the radio suddenly went quiet. "*Nu?* We've arrived. I wish you all the best. Shalom," the driver said.

I helped Lotzi out of the cab and onto his feet, turning my back on the dust cloud that rose up from the wheels as they sped away. Step-by-step, we inched our way forward, Lotzi's weightless arm in mine, a slender bone picked clean of the flesh that had once protected it. At the building's front door he removed a folded envelope from his pocket and a key from inside it. "This is the one," he said, turning it a hundred different ways before it slid into place.

I would have helped Lotzi up a dozen flights of stairs if it meant getting to Yair. But there were only two, and that was hard enough. I took Lotzi's hand, then his elbow, then his shoulder. By the time we reached the top, my arms were wrapped around his body like a brace and did not want to let go.

We stood in front of a door that could have been any door in the world, and neither of us knocked; we just stood there silently, willing it to open of its own accord. After Lotzi returned to himself, he placed the key in my hand and gestured for me to put it to use. "Open it," he said, in case I didn't understand.

But I wasn't ready to open it. I put my arm around Lotzi again. "So he's your son," I said.

"My son," Lotzi confirmed. He nodded once, then opened the door himself.

Together we walked inside, looked around, breathed in the emptiness.

We sat at the kitchen table but did not eat. We sat long enough for me to understand what it meant to be one kind of a survivor and have a son who is another. I knew Lotzi would keep the virus at bay until Yair came home.

When it became clear that his son would not return before nightfall, Lotzi reached into his pocket and pulled out a knife the size of his index finger. "Please, a glass of water," he said.

I cut the onion into small pieces, then added a cucumber and a tomato to it the way Yair had done only a few days before. I waited for Lotzi to count the cucumbers on my fork and say, "He's safe," but he didn't look like a man who wanted to play games. With the feverish fire spreading across his face he looked like his son, but not in the eyes, where it really mattered. The resemblance stopped there.

Lotzi's fork shook in his hands as if it had a life of its own. When he had cleaned his plate, he looked up at me and said, "I'll take a pillow and a few shirts. Maybe some dishes. That's all I need."

At that point, I was still a girl in love, crossing the days off the calendar in my mind. There were only three left. "That's all you need for what?"

"To remember him."

We gathered these things and called a taxi to take us home. I did not tell Lotzi that in three days his son would return and ask for everything back—the pillow we had shared, the shirts I had never seen, the salad bowls still smelling of onion. I did not tell him that a fever as high as his could make a person say things he might later regret.

The old man carried me the whole way down.

Flight

Kyo was waiting outside the practice room to accompany me to lunch, just as he waited every morning to accompany me to breakfast, or to class, or to the conservatory, where he often stood within earshot for the duration of my lesson, the cast of his shadow silhouetted against the door. Once, in the middle of an egregiously bad lesson, I ran out crying and Kyo's arms were already open to catch me; he had even brought tissues with him and held one out as we fled the building under cover of the first lines of Ligeti's "Pour Irina" flowing from the last open door in the hallway. If the scene had not been so pathetic, it would have been romantic, and doubtless was for Kyo, who had foreseen its unfolding the moment my audition for private lessons had been met with approval two weeks earlier—a scene even more painful than the one just described, with snot trickling down my nose. "My best to your father," Professor Auerbach had called as I fled, which made me flee even faster, knowing that strings had been pulled to seat me in front of that Steinway, and that I would never be able to cut them loose. A few days later I was granted a student teacher, an honor accorded to only the most promising of non-music majors.

"You sounded really good in there," Kyo said, sprinting alongside me toward the kosher co-op.

The day was like any other. Frisbees sailed over our heads as we slowed down; a group of students sat in the grass, engaged in a communal back rub and discussion of Heidegger; there was some chanting in the air and some lovemaking I had to step over; but I was far enough away from the Con not to be burdened by the sight of a cello case or the sound of an aria seeping through the walls of that supposedly soundproof place for the hundredth time.

"That student teacher is almost as intimidating as Auerbach," I said, and shuddered.

Kyo stared at me blankly, but I think he understood. I was blaming the teacher, and not myself, for my bad performance. Being my usual self.

"You sounded good. You shouldn't have stopped in the middle."

"Shouldn't have started, you mean. Do you want to stay for lunch?"

"I've got class now. I'll come by your room later."

Kyo would go to the greatest lengths for me as long as they stopped short of the kosher co-op door. He was confused enough about who he was—the "Kyo" half of him often eclipsed by the "Pickering" half—without having to answer to a group of people who lived for the question of who they were.

"Are you sure?"

"I'm sure."

Inside, the Jews were at it again—that is, Danny, the most visible Jew among the kosher co-oppers, with his black velvet *kippah* and wispy beard, was already retaliating one of the daily assaults on his identity, delaying our lunch by several critical minutes.

"You're a self-hater and an *epikorus*," he accused Amalia, as the last of her curls bounced back into place.

"That's a lame rebuttal if I've ever heard one," Amalia replied. She tightened her grip on the spatula we needed to serve ourselves and took a seat beside Danny at the wooden table reserved for the really smart ones among us. The rest of us made do with plastic. "I'm merely positing that if God can't know individuals, as Spinoza claims, he also can't hear your prayers."

"To whom, then, do I daven three times a day?"

"To a God who doesn't know you, and couldn't care less."

"So you think that's a syllogism."

At the challenge of that big word, Amalia's eyes lit up and she released the spatula. "I think prayer makes as much sense as separating linen from wool."

"The commandment of *shatnez* is no less important than honoring your father and mother. Or does that not speak to you either?"

As I listened with one ear, an internal voice caught hold of my other and wouldn't let go. "What's for lunch?" it compelled me to ask out loud, not because I was hungry but because it was the only way to gain entrée into a conversation where I had nothing to contribute. Danny's eyes were upon me then, his need for intellectual engagement temporarily suspended while he tried to figure me out.

"Tuna," he said agreeably.

"Seared?"

"That would be nice. Sandwiches, I'm afraid."

His inquisitive eyes were narrowed now, vaguely in search of a subtext. *Seared* was the best that I could do, and it was better than the last time, when a discussion of Levinas compelled me to tap out a Bach sinfonia on the table, causing a stack of pancakes to tip over. But it was not enough.

"Let it be sandwiches," I said, and threw my arms out in the most Jewish way I knew how, which is to say not at all, having grown up in Indiana. The act was paramount to announcing myself as the empty vessel Danny must have taken me for, just another mouth to feed in an ever-hungrier world.

Touching the top of his head, he adjusted his kippah. "*Ken y'hi ratzon,*" he said, agreeably again; and whatever the hell that meant, it was enough for Amalia to unleash her curls and demand that Danny take back everything he had insinuated about her parents' divorce over breakfast. Nobody took a moment's pause when I whisked myself out of the room.

Sensing the fragile state I was in, Kyo had timed my second flight of the day perfectly, appearing right where he had let me off less than an hour before, at the bottom of the co-op stairs, the only added prop a freshly delivered crate of broccoli by his feet.

"Didn't you have class?" I said, feigning surprise at his presence.

"I left early," Kyo explained.

"Very early."

"It was just review for the test."

We continued our walk through the quad. The air was saturated with the smell of lunch, the same fried cafeteria fare consumed by college students all across America, and a daily reminder that signing up for the kosher co-op had probably been a bad idea, given my love of hash browns and lemon meringue pie.

"What's a syllogism, anyway?" I asked.

"A syllogism?" Kyo's face was suddenly as red as mine had been a few minutes earlier. He was a good student whose parents made him pay every penny of his tuition for not being a better one. I should have known not to transfer my shame onto him, but the strength of our relationship rested on Kyo's resilience in the face of my failures; he was just doing his job. "Hm. I'm not really sure."

"I missed the whole point of the argument because of that stupid word."

"What was the argument?"

"It's hard to summarize."

A small Israeli flag taped to the pavement came into view, with a chalk-scrawled invitation underneath to "STOMP FREELY!" Kyo led me around it.

"I'd like to give a concert," I said. "And I need your help."

"What kind of concert?" Kyo asked.

"Piano, of course. I want to perfect one piece and perform it for a friend."

"What friend?"

"Danny. You don't know him."

"The one with the beanie?"

"You can't be serious."

"Sorry. *Yamaka*."

"It sounds a lot less Japanese if you just say *kippah.* Look, I can't work with that student teacher. 'Ilya'—what kind of guy's name is that, anyway? I want you to teach me that piece you've been playing in the lounge every night."

"The Bach concerto?"

"But not the fast movement."

"OK," said Kyo. "The legato is pretty easy."

I waited for him to ask me about the concert part again, and why it was limited to a single guest. When the time came, Danny might also want to know, though my daily fumblings in his presence had probably already made things pretty clear.

"Great," I said. "So when can we start? And I don't have to pay you, do I? Because I get two credits for studying with Ilya."

"You don't have to pay me," Kyo said. "But you have to let me come to the performance."

"Of course," I said, silently cursing him for always figuring out a way to harmonize the erratic rhythms of my heart with the steady beat of his own. "I can't ask Danny to be the page turner."

*

My piano teachers over the years had been extraordinary musicians, all protégés of Menahem Pressler, whose accent my parents found irresistible. Of these three teachers, I owe my biggest debt of gratitude to Anne-Marie, who kept her hands busy during our lessons with my mother's carob squares and mugs of Cafix, rather than raising them against me as I played. At the end of each lesson, Anne-Marie and I would switch places, and the musical stutterings that had filled the room over the past hour would suddenly make way for a burst of clarity as my teacher took the reins of whatever pieces I had been assigned that week to master, and mastered them.

Under Joseph Ratner, I fared less well. He stopped me at the second measure of a Bach sinfonia only a few minutes after he had introduced himself. "If there are four beats to a measure, how many beats does each eighth note get?" he inquired.

I remained silent, hands in lap. Anne-Marie had never asked such a question.

"Well?"

The question seemed to involve only the numbers four and eight, and I was already in middle school.

"What is one-half of one-fourth?" Ratner ratcheted up the pressure.

"Um . . ."

"You don't know what one half of one fourth is?"

As Ratner rephrased his cruel question again and again ("How many years have you been playing piano? Are you able to read music at all?"), the era of Anne-Marie came to an abrupt and bitter end—all those glorious sounds that had been suspended in a permanent halo above the piano were suddenly bottled up and corked and tossed into the sea. I hated my new piano teacher then, hated his long reptilian fingers and two red tufts of hair, which I suspected held the key to his bad humor. But most of all I hated myself for having falsely believed I was someone's protégé, and that talent came automatically with a good teacher. And now that I had *this* teacher, well, it made me wonder what the point was of letting music into one's life at all.

*

In our dormitory's lounge, I tried to ignore the intimacy of Kyo in his socks and get right down to business.

"Did you bring the music?" I asked, gesturing to his empty hands.

"Of course. It's already at the piano."

Sight-reading is never easy, but with Kyo next to me on the bench, my hands had nowhere to turn but inward, which is how I played until my mind got used to his breath on my neck, lighter than Ilya's but with a strange lulling effect that made the few bookworms in the lounge appear as mannequins in a store window, rather than people whose permission I should have secured before striking the keys.

"This isn't as hard as I thought it would be," I said, gaining confidence midway through the first page. "I've heard you play it so many times, I can predict what's coming next. Bach wouldn't take that the wrong way, would he?"

"You sound great," Kyo confirmed.

"That's what you said last time. And then you handed me a tissue."

"Well, it's true. You're playing it just how Bach wanted, except for those few F-naturals that you read as sharps. There was a key signature change in the second line."

As I took the piece from the top, our lesson took an unexpected turn. Perhaps he thought the competing stimuli in the room would cover it up, or maybe the intoxicating slur of the legato liberated him from thinking at all, but while I played, Kyo allowed a sound to escape from his throat that rose and fell according to the dictates of the music, but with a voice all its own, like a viceroy vying for power.

"What are you doing?" I asked, taking my fingers off the keys.

"Nothing," Kyo said. "What do you mean?"

"You're humming, just like Glenn Gould."

"I am?"

"But you're not humming what I'm playing. You're adding a harmony to it or something."

"Oh. Sorry about that."

But he had a lot more than apologizing to do, for when we rose from the bench and walked out of the room, Kyo's breath was still on my neck, his humming still in my head.

"I want you to come with me to the co-op for Shabbat dinner tomorrow," I announced in the hallway..

"Why?" Kyo wondered, rightly.

"For the chicken and challah," I lied, and then quickly added, "and to meet Danny."

Kyo should have known how to respond to that insensitive offer—in the affirmative. But the lesson had emboldened him.

"I don't know what you see in him," he said.

"It's not what I see in him. It's what I want him to see in me," I said, surprising myself with that sudden insight. "That's what the lessons are for, right?"

"I guess so," said Kyo.

"So see you tomorrow at seven?"

"OK."

*

Rabbi Brenner's sermon was nearing completion when Kyo walked into the co-op the following evening and sat down, completing the circle that distinguished Friday nights from the rest of the rectangular week.

"Being a Jew has never been easy," Rabbi Brenner was saying. "But whereas in the past, it was infighting that led to our ruin—and here I am reminded of the words of Flavius Josephus, who observed, on the eve of the destruction of the Temple in Jerusalem, that the internal divisions of the Jews were more firmly established than the city walls—today we suffer from divisions within ourselves, divisions that cause us to question how comfortable we are in our Jewish skins."

Kyo stared at his hands and scratched an itch. I forced myself not to feel it.

"Therefore, as we embrace the diversity around us, so must we embrace ourselves, beginning with that much-maligned word we are loath to use without its watering-down suffix—the *-ish* that reduces us to a mere religion, rather than a great civilization. Now is the time to reclaim the totality of our existence, by saying, in a voice loud and clear, 'I am a Jew.' OK, folks, everyone sit up straight. Amalia, let's start with you."

Kyo was already sitting up straight, his default position.

"Don't worry," I whispered to Kyo a little too loudly. "You don't have to say it."

"Of course he does," said the rabbi.

"I am a Jew," Kyo announced softly, next in line.

"But he's not," I protested.

"So you don't have to say it," the rabbi clarified. "You want to say something else?"

"Not really," said Kyo.

It was a moment I would rather forget, like when my history paper had been handed back earlier that day, with a big red *C* scrawled at the top and a single line taking issue with a single word I had chosen, describing the Holocaust as "incomprehensible." "Historical analysis requires moving beyond high school clichés," Professor Leonard had written, confirming what I already knew: that I was not cut out for a top-tier liberal arts college and would never take another class of his again. But thanks to the Bach still coursing through my veins, I was able to smile at Leonard's comment, rather than tear it up.

"Why did you say it?" I rasped at Kyo, then rose from my chair and pulled him out of the room and into the kitchen, where bottles of sickly sweet Manischewitz sat alongside two monstrous trays of oversalted chicken in a display that I didn't know whether to take pride in or to apologize for.

"I thought you wanted me to." He shrugged.

"Now you have to unsay it."

"I'm not Jewish," said Kyo.

"I'm not *a Jew*," I corrected.

"I'm not *a Jew*. It's weird, I always thought that was a bad word."

We went back inside to eat, and to meet Danny, who was sitting at the head of the table, arguing with Amalia.

"But it was Hur who tried to stop the golden calf from being built. Why should we remember his mother?"

"Because it was Miriam who instilled those values in him."

"What values? He attacked and was attacked in return. Besides, what were Miriam and all the other women doing with so much jewelry? The calf wasn't made out of clay, you know."

"God, you really should have gone to Binghamton."

"Hi, Danny," I said. It was a greeting like any other.

"Hi, Elissa," Danny said.

Except that I kept going. "It's funny that you should be talking about Jewish mothers," I said. "Because when Rabbi Tarphon's mother lost her sandal, her son put his hands under her feet for the rest of the way home, prompting Rabbi Akiva to later scold his friend for not doing more to help her." I took a breath. "Right?"

Danny turned in his chair just enough to block Amalia completely from view.

"That's exactly right," he said, showing me every one of his straight, white teeth. "Tarphon did not reach even half the obligation of a son to his mother required by the Torah."

I nodded, but I really didn't care. He'd seen that I

had done my homework. If need be, I was also prepared to talk about Caleb the spy and the first few rungs of Jacob's ladder.

"Well, here comes the chicken," I said, and took Kyo to a part of the table that would render Danny invisible for the rest of the evening.

"I thought you wanted me to meet him," Kyo said.

"You just did," I explained. "Isn't he great?"

"When are you going to invite him to the recital?"

"Is there any rush?"

"I think we should have it soon."

"OK," I said. I was glad to have Kyo on my side, rooting for this relationship-in-the-making.

"When do you think I'll be ready?" I asked.

"By next week," Kyo said. "But we have to practice hard."

"It's a deal. But on one condition."

"What's that?"

To avoid unnecessary eye contact, I poured myself some Manischewitz. "No more humming."

*

Things remained business as usual between us. Every day Kyo escorted me to my classes, helped me with my homework, and indulged my cravings for beef jerky, which could be bought only at a single gas station a mile from campus, and by running very fast across a highway. But one evening before our lesson, I heard that humming again and, following it into the lounge, found Kyo at the piano, engaged in some kind of covert operation.

"You're more slouched over than Gould ever was," I said, standing next to him. "Don't stop. Keep playing."

But he had already stopped. "Is it time for class already?" he asked, glancing at the watch on his wrist.

"Yours or mine?"

"You have poetry now. Did you finish your Donne paper?"

"Done. My dad dictated most of it to me over the phone."

"But I liked your analysis," Kyo said.

"Well, he didn't."

Kyo was in a peculiar mood that morning; rather than letting me speak for the both of us, he appeared bent on not letting me speak at all, filling in each step we took with a new and colorful revelation, like a gardener planting flowers he had grown from seeds.

"I reserved a hall for the recital," he began.

"You did? Is it—"

"Kulas, not Warner. Since we're only seating one."

"Couldn't we just have it in a practice ro—"

"The acoustics in Kulas are amazing. Remember the Beethoven concert we went to during orientation week?"

"I remember the Snickers bar I ate at intermi—"

"You claimed you could play the *Moonlight Sonata* better than Evgeny Kissin, and that he needed a haircut."

"I didn't say I could play it better. I said my teacher Anne-Marie c—"

"And I think you could, if you put your mind to it like you're doing with the Bach. I think you could play it better than anyone."

I should have stopped him then. I should have thrown up my hand midsentence, said, "Whoa, slow down, horsie!" canceled the recital, and quit college, which was becoming a bigger burden every day, like a stain that a wipe-down only makes worse.

Instead I said, "Go on."

"I reserved the hall for this Thursday at seven," Kyo said, "and Danny promised he wouldn't be late."

"Danny? When did you—"

"After dinner, when Amalia was trying to rope you into that women's study group. He seemed happy to get the invitation—he didn't even know that you played piano. Why didn't you ever tell him? That's the first thing a guy wants to know about a girl."

"You mean the first thing *you* wa—"

"Anyway, now he knows. And he promised not to be late."

*

I was nearly catatonic when I entered Kulas on Thursday evening at 6:45 p.m., my nerves having left me in a state of virtual numbness. I consequently registered nothing when I spotted Kyo on the stage, decked out in a polo shirt and starched pants, and then Danny a moment later sitting in the first row, hands clasped and resting on a bouncing knee.

I tried to snap out of it by breaking with performance protocol. "Are we ready to roll?" I asked, waving at Danny as a way to warm up my ice-cold hands.

"This is pretty cool," said Danny, surveying the room

and not seeming to mind at all that the evening was dedicated to him. And it was cool, the even dispersion of our voices setting the mood before the music even began. So cool that, for a moment, I thought I might just dispense with going onstage at all, and run home.

"It's seven o'clock," Kyo announced. "Let's start."

The stage was big, and I hadn't noticed the second piano on it, which Kyo rolled from the side to the center, as if reconnecting two Siamese twins who had been separated at birth.

"That's OK, I'm fine with the other one," I said, and sat down.

"But I'm not," Kyo said with a firmness that made my hands freeze all over again. He took out a bundle of music and sat at the second piano.

"What are y—"

"Here's your part." He handed me my music. "Do you mind turning the pages yourself?"

"I don't mind."

"Great. And don't forget to tell Danny what we're playing."

I looked askance at those angled walls of Kulas, and then at Kyo, smiling at the sabotage under way. "The legato movement of Bach's Concerto in C Minor?"

"Bach's Concerto in C Minor for Two Pianos," he corrected me, patting his own part as if it were a well-behaved child. "That cool with you, Danny?"

"Sure," Danny said.

It was a betrayal of the most beautiful kind, Kyo's two hands mirroring my every move while I played, superimposing his own voice onto the one I had been saving for Danny, and for Danny alone. For the first few minutes I stayed close to the keys, hoping to throw my adversary off with restraint and bring him back to his senses. I tried to summon Rabbi Brenner ushering in the Sabbath with his *bim bim bam* song rising up from his belly to silence the Bach at a single blow, and then Danny arguing with Amalia—the cacophony of an average day at college. And when the humming started, I tried even harder, conjuring two giant cotton balls that would render me as deaf as Beethoven if only they could find a way into my ears.

But music has a life of its own, and Kyo and I sounded so good together. For Danny's sake, I had arrived in T-shirt and jeans to emphasize that his laws of modesty applied to me as well; soon my outfit was drenched in sweat. Kyo and I played passionately until the bitter end, two slaves singing the song of their master to set themselves free. When the piece was over, Danny clapped for a long time, as if he too had something to say, or maybe to remind us of his presence in the hall. Then he asked us if we wouldn't mind taking it from the top and playing it again.

A Foggy Day

When I was eighteen years old, I took a bus to a sad place. Across from me sat a mother and her baby. While the mother read a newspaper, the child drank from her droopy breast, a stream of milk trickling out the sides of his mouth onto the seat below. I watched, trying to remember if I had ever been that thirsty, lips dry and cracked from dehydration. I could not remember a single time.

The bus made a sharp turn and I turned with it, bending just far enough to brush the edge of a man's arm. "Oops," I apologized. "That was a big one." Startled, the man shifted his arm, examined it, and then let it drop carelessly to his side. When the bus leveled out again, I settled back into place and stared out the window.

Outside, the world was engaged in conversation. I tried to read the signs on people's lips as we lumbered by. With the help of gestures I made out greetings, curses, inquiries, and exhortations. Repeating the greetings to myself elicited more greetings; curses, more curses. When I asked my neighbor for the time, he answered me only in numbers.

Nobody was waiting for me at the last stop. I looked in each direction to make sure. Five years earlier, my piano teacher had waited for me here once a week. Now he was waiting for someone else, at a different stop. A vendor stood behind a pushcart, selling pretzels. One of his arms was looped with pretzels while the other turned the pages of a magazine. I bought a pretzel from his wrist. Before putting it in a bag, he gave it a spin and sang a short rhyming song.

I was not happy with my surroundings. The farther I walked, the less happy I became. After a stretch, I tried to sing the vendor's song but could remember only the rhymes and not the rhythm. *Oom*-pah-pah? *Oom*-pah-*oom*? Pah-*oom*-pah? Suddenly I was back at the sad place, at the spot where my piano teacher had picked me up once a week and led me to his studio. While he made haste, I would lag behind to watch the way he walked, and to make sure I did not walk that way myself.

Once, before a lesson, I spied a single doughnut, perfectly round, sitting on the coffee table in the studio. While my teacher adjusted the piano bench, I scooped up the doughnut and shoved it into my mouth. My mouth was too small and I could barely breathe, but it was my fingers I was worried about, which could not be licked clean no matter what. My teacher sniffed the air with satisfaction before he sat down.

The lesson always began with a game. My teacher would ask me a question about the piano, and I would answer it.

"Who invented the piano?"

"I don't know."

"How many strings are on a typical piano?"

"I don't know."

"Is a grand piano constructed on a vertical or horizontal plane?"

"Vertical?"

After the game, I played a series of scales. When my fingers moved up the keyboard, my teacher leaned to the right. When they moved down the keyboard, he swung to the left. I was not comfortable with scales; each note followed the next in such quick succession, there was no time to correct a mistake. My teacher explained that unlike in scales, a wrong note in a chord will make a new and different chord. I asked him whether I could play chords instead of scales. He said no.

In the middle of my fifth scale, I saw my teacher's eyes shift from the piano to the coffee table. I followed them until they landed on the empty plate where the doughnut had been, then felt my palms grow moist and my fingers cold. Almost immediately my teacher pulled out a page of notes and asked me to play Chopin.

I stumbled through one nocturne after another, my teacher keeping time with his foot and nodding in approval. When my fingers moved up the keyboard, he leaned to the left; when they moved down, he leaned even farther. Soon I could feel his breath on my neck, and the music came out stiff and rigid, like the bench I was sitting on.

After the lesson, I asked my teacher whether I could play something less serious next time, maybe Gershwin or Bach. He asked me what I meant by serious. I shrugged and said I didn't know.

On the bus ride home that day I thought about the way my teacher walked, his feet turned inward as though following some podiatric pull of gravity. I stood up to make sure my own feet had not succumbed to the same force and began to walk down the aisle of the bus.

The angle of my feet widened with each step I took. By the time I reached the front of the bus, I was ready to walk the rest of the way home.

My neighbor, a Holocaust survivor from Hungary, was standing outside her apartment on the first floor, fumbling with a key. When she saw me she pushed at the door with her shoulder until it opened, then pulled me inside. "Do you know that my husband died?" she said. "Almost fifty years now."

Later that afternoon I tried to imagine what it would be like to have a husband who had been dead for fifty years. Every year another number, every number another death. I turned on the radio and hoped Mrs. Marmerstein could hear it. I laid my forehead against the door and counted rhythms and beats. If she had to count, this was the best way to do it. I looked around for a fourth note to add to the basic three-note chord of the song and found it in the heel of my shoe.

When I returned to my piano teacher's studio the following week, a doughnut was sitting on the coffee table again, chocolate-covered and conspicuous. I brushed by it like a stranger and took my seat stiffly at the piano.

I waited for my teacher to tell me what to play, but his mind appeared to be elsewhere. "Are you thinking of questions to ask me?" I said. "Because I never know any of the answers."

My teacher straightened in his chair and told me to start with Chopin, the *n* emerging from his mouth in a silent stream of air. I placed my fingers on the keyboard, pretending his was a reasonable request.

In the middle of the first page I felt a weight on my

shoulder. I shook it off and continued to play. By the beginning of the second page, knuckles were kneading my spine. I withdrew my fingers from the keyboard and feigned a forceful sneeze.

Before I could continue playing, the question game commenced. Resting his hand on my arm, my teacher asked, "Does this bother you?"

I shrugged hard and his hand fell away. "No, no," I said politely.

He placed the palm of his hand on the small of my back. "How about this?"

I laughed, then coughed, then sneezed again.

"Listen," I said, forcing my fingers back onto the keys. "Gershwin. 'A Foggy Day.'"

My teacher watched as I played. One wrong note after the other. "Try an arpeggio," he suggested.

"Arpeggios don't work in 'A Foggy Day,'" I lied. "Because of the syncopation."

After "A Foggy Day" I played "My Gal Sal" and "Jingle Bells." Then a few waltzes and a mazurka. When I was through, I stood up and thanked my teacher for the lesson. "I've got to catch the bus before it leaves," I apologized. "There's only one bus that I can ride."

On the walk that day, I turned around every few feet to check if my teacher was following me.

On the bus I turned to the man sitting next to me to see if it was my teacher.

At home I knocked on Mrs. Marmerstein's door to see if my teacher would answer it. Mrs. Marmerstein answered. "I'm just putting on the *tshaynik* for a cup of tea," she said. "Come in."

I came in. Together we sat at her kitchen table, sipping tea from chipped porcelain cups. I wanted to know something about Mrs. Marmerstein.

"Do you have any children?" I asked.

"I have you," she said, refilling my cup.

When I stood to leave, she held my face in her hands and kissed the top of my head. "Do you know that my husband died?" she asked, tears streaming down her cheeks. "Almost fifty years now."

That night I lay in bed, counting sheep. They came in big flocks, a hundred at a time. Other people might have been having trouble sleeping then too—my piano teacher, the pretzel vendor, Mrs. Marmerstein for sure. But I was probably the only one counting. When the rhymes from the pretzel vendor's song started to interfere with my exercise, I tried to shoo them away, but could not. *Mellow* and *fellow, moon* and *soon, summertime* and *baby mine*—they filled my head like the music they were a part of, and I did not want music in my life anymore, not even a pretzel vendor's ditty. With great willpower I herded the sheep back to me and let them come until I could count no higher. Fifty thousand, one hundred thousand, a million and more. A pool of saliva formed at the edge of my pillow. I turned my head and swam the other way.

Thinking in Third Person

I had tried so hard to think in third person, and with the mind of a man. But I kept coming back to myself, a woman whose loneliness had led her to long intervals of sleep and then more inward still, to a registration form for ballroom dancing and a pen full of ink. I filled it out, but I didn't go. I sent my husband instead. Now he not only dances but also plays the accordion. It's a good development for us both, even if it hasn't brought me out of bed and into the world.

In the meantime, in Tel Aviv, sand sweeps through the city from the Horn of Africa and settles on the surface of Elhanan Schweitzer's coffee cup. Schweitzer's coffee catches between his teeth but he pretends not to notice, turning his face toward the wind and swallowing hard, as if reburying a sorrow that has risen after a long sleep. He is glad about this sudden change in weather and has to suppress a laugh at the displeasure on the faces of his fellow Zorik Café patrons, their eyes reduced to near slits, faulty screens that shield against only the largest particles. I'm not Schweitzer, but I can feel his schadenfreude, the day-old stubble on his cheeks—or probably it's the sand—and his happiness about the haze that frees him from acknowledging his wife, standing across the street under an umbrella and beckoning him back home. The wind pulls the words out of her mouth before they are fully formed.

My husband is a passionate lovemaker. He understands that to enjoy the compromised life we live in this small town, we must carve out a parallel life in a universe of our own making—that is, of his own making but with my permission. Last night he pulled me to a sitting position, then to a standing one. On the bed. I knew what was coming next and didn't resist at first. I am grateful for Jonathan's ingenuity, for giving me reasons to open my eyes at the close of days I think will never end, at the end of which I want to go on and on. Jonathan whispered in my ear: "Keep your shoulder parallel and your thigh locked. I'll do everything else."

With my husband pressed against me, I wanted the day to go on and on. But when he raised his foot and expected me to do the same, my body froze.

"What are you doing?"

"*Shh.* Diagonally forward on the L toe. Just keep your cheek close to mine, that's right, just like that. Up on the toe just a little more. Now lower your heel, and left sway."

Our alternate universe was not nearly as big as it needed to be. "I can't, Jonathan. I don't want to. You know I don't know how to dance—"

"Who said anything about dancing?"

Rising to the balls of his feet, Jonathan entered me then, a surprise move to keep me from falling back down onto the bed and into a missionary position. "We almost did a curved feather," he whispered. "But this is much better, isn't it? I love you so much, Mira."

"Yes, it is," I whispered back. And it was, because

some passions are meant to be kept separate. I went to sleep feeling sorry for both Schweitzer and his wife.

*

When Schweitzer returns home, a woman twenty years younger than his wife is standing in the kitchen, washing dishes.

"Where's Tova?" Schweitzer asks.

"She flew to Czernowitz this morning," the woman says, a blond bun pinned to the top of her head like a bauble. "I'm Leona. Sit down and I'll give you some soup."

Schweitzer sits. "But I just saw her, at the café."

"It must have been someone else," says Leona. "Who can make out anyone in all this dust?"

"Why Czernowitz?"

"To clean her grandparents' graves. In Czernowitz, at least, the dust has a purpose."

"Is that what she said?"

Leona had hoped to take credit for the statement. "That's what she said."

Schweitzer eats his soup as he had drunk his coffee, with sand between his teeth and a frailty laid bare by forces of nature that are beyond his control. The only thing he feels he can still reasonably do without a fight is eat from a jar of olives with a toothpick. He suddenly has a craving.

"If you don't mind, the olives." Schweitzer motions to the fridge. The toothpicks are already on the table.

With soapy fingers, Leona hands him the jar, easily

suppressing an urge to ask whether the soup needs more salt, because she really doesn't care.

"The soup is fine," Schweitzer says preemptively, as if his wife were standing before him. And then—stabbing a kalamata—to Leona: "I don't often get to eat olives this way. My wife says that small pleasures often lead to great sorrows. That one day I'll swallow the toothpick."

The old man misses his wife, thinks Leona bitterly.

How good it feels to defy Tova, thinks Schweitzer, and helps himself to another olive.

*

In Czernowitz, Tova is offered a tour of the city by her taxi driver, free of charge. She turns him down.

My Czernowitz isn't your Czernowitz. She is surprised by such a thought coming to her, a Haifa native with a grandson in the army.

"I'm just here to visit the cemetery," Tova says. "I live in Israel."

"Israel," repeats the driver. He feels a faint throbbing at his temples. Cracks the window.

My grandparents lived in Czernowitz, Tova continues to herself. *Together with the Yiddishists and the Bundists, the Hassids, the assimilationists and Zionists. Who could leave such a place? Who could kill such people?*

"They were the lucky ones. They have graves," Tova hears herself say. But it is really her mother speaking, and she wishes she had kept her mouth shut. That both of them had kept their mouths shut.

The driver lights a cigarette. He can't wait to get this

woman out of his cab. And for free he had offered the tour! But that was before he knew where she was going. Never again will he let his boredom get the better of him.

They arrive at the crumbling wall of the cemetery. The graves mirror the inside of the driver's mouth. He turns off the meter, which reads "50 РУБЛИ." "One hundred rubles," the driver dares himself to say. And then he says it.

Tova pays, adding a tip. She doesn't want any anti-Semites on her conscience. She thanks the driver and steps out of the cab.

*

"That's right, my friend Georg is a monarchist," Jonathan confirms. We are sitting on a bench in the park, holding hands.

"But what does that mean, exactly?" Little birds dance around us that I don't recognize but that Jonathan easily identifies as sparrows. It has been quite a while since I have been out.

"Well, as long as there is still a living von Habsburg, the idea of reestablishing the monarchy can be embraced by lunatics like Georg, who doesn't even have his own apartment."

"And are there?"

"Are there what?"

"Still-living von Habsburgs."

"Otto died last year, but I think Karl is still around. According to Georg, Karl hosts a game show."

It's hard to take in so much information without being able to pull up the covers and process it in a state of deep sleep. "Czernowitz was part of the Austro-Hungarian Empire," I say, dreamily.

"Yes, it was," Jonathan says. "Along with other minorities of the time, the Jews fared pretty well under the kaiser. That's why so many of them hung Franz Joseph's portrait in their living rooms."

"And that's why Georg wants the monarchy back? So we can all get along?"

"Something like that," says Jonathan. "But mostly he just wants to show off at parties."

I squeeze Jonathan's hand in gratitude. The tutorial will help Tova as she sits with pieces of her grandparents' tombstones on her lap. They have broken since her last visit and are no longer covered with moss. Where she couldn't before, she can now read the names clearly: Wolf and Ella Meyerson. Tova can't imagine two names sounding nicer together.

At home Jonathan practices his accordion while I prepare an elaborate Indian meal almost without thinking, as if I have been preparing elaborate Indian meals all my life. On a recent visit, my mother brought with her an exchange student, who spent five days teaching me the secrets of her country's cuisine while my mother sat on the couch, knitting a scarf. It was all so surreal that I can pretend these five days didn't actually happen at all, and that I am simply a gifted cook. Because, really, who would do that, ride on a train for eighteen hours with my mother, rather than remind her that the airport is only a mile away?

The kitchen is smoking with spices when Schweitzer peers into the umbrella barrel by the door. "It's empty," he says to Leona. "My wife's umbrella is gone."

"Your wife is in Czernowitz," Leona repeats for what feels like the hundredth time. "Why wring your hands with worry?" She wishes Schweitzer would get tired so she could let her hair down and watch TV.

But Schweitzer is neither tired nor worried. Plucking his hat from its peg, he prepares to leave, to go back out into the storm and look for the woman shouting wildly against the wind. He is sure it was his wife standing on the sidewalk across from Zorik's, bent under her umbrella. The proof is in the empty barrel. And if not his wife, then another woman in great need of his attention. Schweitzer is ready to listen now. He hopes the storm will last long enough to let him.

Alone in the apartment, Leona loosens her hair but does not turn on the TV. Where *is* Czernowitz? she wonders for the first time since making arrangements with Tova. In Russia? Then why had she never heard of it as a child? In Poland, maybe, or somewhere in Hungary? Before she left, Tova had asked Leona if she knew any words of Ruthenian and Leona had laughed, thinking it a joke. What was Ruthenian and why would she know it? Leona felt like an object of ridicule, that people were always putting her down. Where was Czernowitz, and why did her husband so often come home from work wet? *Because my clients like to swim,* he would say, shrugging, *and we live in a country where deals are closed in the middle of the sea.*

No, she didn't know any German either. Not a word. *Shut up, lady! Go to Czernowitz already. Zay gezunt.*

It is not too late to become an audiologist. The voice of Leona's husband rings in her ears. *There is still time to follow your dreams.*

Yiddish, of course! Tova had exclaimed in parting, throwing up her hands. *As a last resort, I can always use Yiddish.* And Leona had laughed again.

Meanwhile, farther north at Metula, Schweitzer's nephew Yair, performing the magic of a monarchist, protects the border with a pair of binoculars.

*

The key to dispelling loneliness is in not letting it come back. I am feeling better about my life when Jonathan walks through the door, trying to hide something behind his back that is not meant to be hidden outside the context of war or a rendezvous.

"Is that a suitcase?" I ask, admiring the wheels.

"Yes," Jonathan says, his eyes even more aglow than usual. "I wanted it to be a surprise, but you're up early today. That is, you're up today."

I stare at the suitcase in earnest now. "Are we going somewhere?"

"Anywhere your heart desires. My dad is sending me all of his frequent-flier miles for my birthday. He's taking my mom on a cruise."

My heart is beating hard; it must desire so much.

"Maybe we can cash them in," I suggest. "I've never owned a laser pen, or anything bound in leather."

"How about Rome?" Jonathan says. "The travel agent said we could get a free rental car if we went to Rome."

"Rome?" I once looked out the window and saw Rome.

"Or how about Tel Aviv?" Jonathan tries. "You've always wanted to go there."

My husband deserves a vacation, and a birthday dinner he will be able to digest. And more than that: we all seek places to go when the people around us start to look the same. But some people are afraid of traveling by conventional means (ask my mother why she took that train), and I have already been to Tel Aviv several times in the past week.

"I don't know, I feel kind of bound to stay here right now, in bed," I say, stretching my limbs casually to conceal my terror. "You know how I am about being in a room with more than four people."

Jonathan sets his hands on my shoulders and I wait for him to shake me, but he does no such thing. "I'll let you think it over, OK?" he says, the very words he once used to woo me.

I rub myself against my husband like a royal cat, grateful for the gift he is giving me, for being allowed to say no.

"You go to Tel Aviv," I suddenly decree. "It will be like when we first met, and I refused to see you for a week. Remember? And take a friend along. How about Purnima? My mother says it's freezing in Skokie."

Jonathan strokes my back and waits for me to come to my senses. I turned him down once before, in the presence of a newly purchased ring, until he agreed to have all of our groceries delivered and to be married in the quiet of a courtroom, where people who have nothing to prove go. We should have had a klezmer band, though. I regret that we didn't.

Brushing past me, my husband parks the suitcase in a corner and picks up the accordion from its place. A mazurka fills the room and ferries him away, as if on a cloud I can't reach. The loneliness is back, and it is unbearable.

"Jonathan? Jonathan!"

I will wait for the music to stop and ask him for the next dance.

The Other Air

I had been sighing a lot. A breath would rise from within me, then slowly release itself, like the failed note from a broken instrument. I took myself to the doctor. On the bus, I watched the driver insert a straw into a bottle of ginger ale. The bottle was too big and swallowed the straw up. At the next light, the driver tipped the bottle until the round plastic stalk bobbed to the surface, then jammed his tongue into the hole. The straw caught, and he drew it out with his teeth. Then he set the bottle in its holder beside the steering wheel and forgot about it.

The doctor came into the room on crutches. He was missing a leg. Without introducing himself he handed me a cardboard tube and told me to blow into it. As I blew, he pointed to a series of fidgeting numbers on a computer, and a jagged orange line climbing steadily across the screen. When it could climb no higher, the doctor assured me that my lungs were in good order, clear and strong, and suggested that my frequent sighing was connected to a heightened emotional state. I stared at the empty space where the doctor's leg should have been and felt a twitch in my knee, as though it had just been tapped with a hammer. I thanked the doctor for his diagnosis.

My mother worked as an immigration lawyer. Every time we spoke on the phone, she had a different accent. Occasionally I would receive a letter from her addressed to me but meant for someone else. I would readdress the letter and send it back in the same envelope. Our correspondence consisted of copying down each other's names like this. The similarity in our handwriting was uncanny.

When I called her, my mother reminded me that I had never been happy as a child, that during the first five years of my life I had fallen into the toilet twice, once with a shiny penny emerging from my bowels. She told me that on her side of the family there was a history of catching one's breath, but that nobody had ever called it sighing. To illustrate her point she described a picture taken many years ago, of my grandmother swimming in the Danube, her face tilted toward the sky as she came up for air. On either side of her a young man reached playfully for her shoulder. One of them would later send my great-grandparents to their deaths, but my mother couldn't remember which.

After I hung up the phone, I went for a walk. As I walked, I tried to summon the face of my boyfriend, whom I had not seen in several days. I closed my eyes and a cluster of floaters clouded my vision, turning my boyfriend's face into damaged goods, his countenance pockmarked with the shadows cast on my retina. Stopping at a building, I climbed a set of stairs in search of something familiar. Rabbi Kogan stood at the door with his arms crossed and led me inside.

His beard was longer than I remembered. I stared at it, wishing it shorter. I said, "Reb Kogan."

Rabbi Kogan nodded. He pointed to a chair stacked with leather-bound tomes. "You've got a difficult question for me today?" he asked hopefully. "Sit. Ask."

"And the books?"

Rabbi Kogan cleared the books from the chair. "Ask a harder question," he said.

While I tried to think of a question, I stared at the rabbi's beard. It was a big beard, thick and black with sporadic strands of gray. The rabbi saw me staring. He said, "A Jew is forbidden to remove even a single white hair from his black beard."

Before I could respond, I felt a cold draft inside me, and a sigh escaped. "Actually, I came to make a donation," I said. "To the disabled."

"Very good, we'll send it to Israel. What else?" Rabbi Kogan asked.

I handed him a twenty-dollar bill. "Nothing else," I said. "I've been sighing a lot, having to catch my breath. It's exhausting. I'd like it to stop."

The rabbi waved the money under my nose like a jar of smelling salts. "You're a Jew, you sigh. It's a fact. Don't try to change it."

At home, I wrote a thank-you note to Dr. Wilson. I wrote, "Dear Dr. Wilson, thank you for seeing me on such short notice today. Best wishes, etc."

The post office was closed, but a small line had formed outside, and I placed myself in it. I read the thank-you note again before sealing the envelope, then watched the man in front of me tear open a package of socks and put them on.

When I was younger I knew a boy named Max, whose parents had named him Max after deciding he should become a grocer. Five years after Max became a grocer, I received an invitation to the opening of his sixtieth store. At the opening, Max led me to his favorite aisle, of canned vegetables and soup mixes. He said, "Have you ever seen so much shit?"

He told me that his parents had envisioned him selling black bread and kipper snacks from a dark room on a residential corner. Their dream was to live upstairs, above the store, and listen to the traffic below, the ring of the cash register, the crunch of a pickle. When a customer couldn't pay in cash, he would be able to pay on credit, the pinnacle of Max's parents' fantasy. At the end of every month, they would descend the creaky stairs to help restock the shelves and smooth out the wrinkles in their son's apron.

"I'll stop at a hundred," he said.

*

I was still sighing. Sometimes I looked into the mirror when I breathed, opened my mouth, and peered inside as the cold air brushed against my gums. I didn't very much like what I saw: two rows of teeth that had resisted years of costly orthodontia and a dark tunnel at the back of my throat through which all of my sighs passed before exiting. There was usually nothing more to do but close my mouth again and wait for the next sigh.

Then my mother called to tell me that my grandmother had died, and that I was to give the eulogy at her funeral.

I thought it was a joke, a horrible misunderstanding. Wasn't my grandmother already dead? Hadn't she suffered a heart attack years ago while waiting for a bus in the middle of winter, after my mother had refused to drive her to the hairdresser?

My mother scolded me for rewriting history. She admitted that we hadn't visited enough, but reminded me that as a child I had scraped the prune filling out of my grandmother's *palatschinken*, cried when a cloud of paprika settled in her hair, screamed when I sat on her knee for stories and the *r*'s came out rolled. "'Just as the dead shall be called to account, so shall the eulogizers be called to account,'" my mother warned me, quoting from the Talmud.

In short, I was to give the eulogy because I had known Magda best.

I prepared for the funeral by seeking comfort in the arms of my boyfriend. First he held me one way, then another, straining his back both times to try to give me the help I needed. When he finally found a comfortable position, I was being cradled like a baby, my legs hanging by his side, limp and useless. "Is this it? Is this how she used to do it?" my boyfriend asked, wanting to get it right. I burrowed deeper into the crook of his arm. "It might be," I said, slowly beginning to feel the strain in my own back. "There are only so many ways to hold a baby."

*

We stopped seven times on our way to the grave. "We pause to reflect upon the vanities often mistaken for a meaningful life," Rabbi Meyer explained. "What is human existence?"

At the grave-side service we tossed spadefuls of earth over the grave. When Rabbi Meyer bent down to pick up a pen that had fallen out of his pocket, everyone bent down. After the kaddish, my mother announced that I wished to say a few words about my grandmother. She turned to me and stroked my face with the back of her rough hand. She said, "We probably should have visited more often."

I stepped forward, out of the tight circle. I looked around. "Bubbe?" I called out. "Magda?" I stepped back into the circle.

Before leaving the cemetery we washed our hands. Rabbi Meyer explained why. "We are clean," he said. "We have done everything in our power to keep the deceased in life, to ease her distress."

I felt my mother's fingers climb up my back like a spider. "At least once a year," she whispered.

My boyfriend was waiting for me in the living room when I came home. He asked, "Why are you so dirty?"

I looked at my feet, caked in mud, and said, "I just buried my grandmother in a deep grave."

We sat in separate chairs. We didn't speak much. Instead we made sounds, pushing the air out of our lungs, then pulling it in again with equal force. Soon my boyfriend was asleep, and my head was spinning with loneliness. I shut my eyes and reached out for something stable. When the room righted itself, I got up to close the door and listen for the sound it always made: the cough of someone waiting to come in.

Amnon

I cannot recite the street names of Tel Aviv by heart because I have not really lived there. And when Amnon stuck his head out the window to ask me to run to the *makolet* for a lemon, it was not the street sign that I was looking at, but Amnon. The absence of window screens in the city allowed me to take him in all at once, unobscured, with nothing between us but the urgency of completing a salad. The cucumbers and tomatoes were already chopped and waiting in the bowl.

I did not know where the *makolet* was, but I followed my instincts and got lost after a single turn. The roads were potholed and sandy, congested with cars and pedestrians all moving in different directions but at the same frenetic pace. At Rothschild Boulevard I slowed down to consider a canopy of trees and two old women sitting on a bench. I wanted them to be speaking Yiddish and they were, so I put the trees aside and considered them instead, getting close enough to smell their face powder and peek into a canvas bag sitting by their feet. More tomatoes and cucumbers.

It was late when I found my way back to Amnon's. In the courtyard of his apartment building stood a small grove of lemon trees, all bearing fruit.

Amnon regarded the lemon in my hand, particularly the white flower and stem still attached from my pulling too hard on the tree, before he looked at me.

"You didn't find the *makolet?*" he asked, glancing at the same window from which he had called down his request an hour before.

"I took the scenic route," I explained. I did not say more but instead reached out for Amnon, to see if we could still manage to complete each other after all this time apart. "It was a long trip, getting here." I meant crossing the ocean as well as having to wrest myself from that bench on Rothschild Boulevard. It is always hard to see Yiddish die, even in the first Hebrew city of Tel Aviv.

Amnon accepted my embrace for exactly three seconds. "I'll get a proper lemon," he said, placing my offering on the table and preparing to run away. "The ones in front—" He shook his head as if I should have known better. "No good."

I should have known *him* better, Amnon; for three months, long ago, we had tilled the same land together, fed the same cows, sewn the same red identification threads onto our work shirts. But without a kibbutz to keep us in concert, one of us was always straying from the other.

"Hurry back," I said.

While he took the stairs two at a time, I tried to bridge the distance between us by setting the table, and when that was done, by standing before the walls of Amnon's apartment and willing them to speak. A reproduction of a Picasso, in cheap poster form, took up the eastern wall; an oversize calendar depicting scenes from old American movies hung on the western side. Neither said a word.

A quiet energy pulled me into the bedroom, first to Amnon's closet, empty but for a few shirts of foreign extraction, and then to a small bookshelf next to his bed with more than a dozen Hebrew books offering me a way in. When Amnon returned with the lemon, I was still struggling with the first title.

We ate on the balcony overlooking another couple eating on their balcony. For most of the first course Amnon conversed with his neighbors, shouting over the traffic and our chewing, the seagulls squawking overhead and live music delivered from Rabin Square. It would not be easy to convince him to leave.

"You know why I'm in Israel," I finally said, as a salty breeze blew over us.

"Yes," Amnon replied. "But now is not a good time to move, and I know nothing of America."

*

There were moments when I felt I could have lived on the kibbutz forever, and they all occurred in Virginia, usually in the morning and in the shower, where I often gave voice to the Zionist folk songs I had learned at summer camp. With every fresh experience on the kibbutz, I threw up. It was all new to me: the desert, the date trees, the ancient wells from which we drew our water to funnel into jerricans and drink in the fields. Even the sun, forcing us to finish our work by midday; I had not previously known it for the foe it was, there in the Arava.

The nurse told me to drink water, and to wear a hat.

She warned me to steer clear of the date thorns, and to hold my breath when a diesel tractor drove by. She did not ask how I felt being penned in with twenty-five other volunteers all from the same country, day and night, in the fields and around the campfires. She did not ask how I'd felt the first time I saw Amnon.

I had been waiting my whole life to love someone, and the kibbutz was a natural place to fall in love, a fertile crescent crafted out of sand. But it was along hard asphalt and not sand that I walked one evening, finding myself at the entrance of the kibbutz, where Amnon sat guard. When I came within a few feet of him, a bright light snapped on between us, and I stopped.

"Something happened?" he asked me in English, his eyes traveling up the road toward the kibbutz.

It seemed a world away, suddenly. "Nothing happened," I assured him, squinting at the light and stepping closer. "I'm just going for a walk."

Instead of offering me his chair, Amnon stood up and laid his gun across it. A whiff of strong soap accompanied him, quickly evaporating into the acacia trees above us. He did not smell like a soldier at all.

"It's a strange place to walk, on a paved road," Amnon observed. "What's your name?"

"Nava."

"Nava?" He looked surprised. "Nava is an Israeli name."

"My parents wanted part of me to always be here," I explained. "Even when I'm back home."

"And when will that be?"

"In three months."

I was eighteen years old then, and waking up at

dawn every morning. To me, three months sounded like a very long time.

Amnon was eighteen too. “Some volunteers stay for a year,” he said, visibly disappointed. “I’m Amnon. Come, I’ll take you for a real walk.”

Slinging the gun across his shoulder, he removed a key from his pocket, and a few seconds later the gates of the kibbutz fell open, revealing a massive expanse of sand that mirrored the state of my young, swelling heart.

In the next three months I did not throw up again.

*

After dinner on the balcony, over wine that I had brought expressly for the occasion, I repeated my offer to Amnon. “You’re unemployed,” I reminded him. “You’re paying a fortune to rent an apartment the size of my closet in Virginia. Just come for the summer, until the situation here improves. My father said he can give you some computer work, and on the weekends we can travel.”

I heard the words distinctly as they came out of my mouth, but from Amnon’s response you wouldn’t have guessed I had spoken at all. “I’m getting a dog,” he announced, as scales from a poorly tuned piano suddenly swept through the open window into the room. “Something small and easy, whatever they have at the pound. There’s a park nearby.”

The disconnect did not deter me. On the contrary, it set me up to state the obvious. “A dog will not protect you, Amnon." I tried to speak above the music without shouting, even when the music stopped and was replaced by shouting. "A dog may not even smell it coming."

Amnon set down his wineglass, took his two hands, and threaded them through his hair. Then he stood up. "Come, I'll take you to the park," he said. "You should have passed it on your way to the *makolet*."

Outside, Amnon's steps were slow and heavy, as if an insistent wind had risen from the sea to push against his feet and force me to make sense of my surroundings.

"Look at all these 'For Sale' signs," I said. We passed one building after another with people waiting to move out. "Everyone can feel it but you."

Amnon picked up his pace a little. Pebbles dislodged by his sandals flew into my shoes. "If the prices were lower, these flats would sell in one day," he said. "They'll probably sell anyway. This is Tel Aviv."

We walked some more—not for long, but for long enough to feel the weight of my thirty years touching down, and of Amnon's close behind. It was a stark contrast to the lightness that lifted me up when I thought of his accompanying me back home.

At the entrance to the park, Amnon stopped and held out his hands as if they were full, and not empty. "Here we are," he said. "Now you'll understand why I want a dog."

I looked around for some traditional signs of a park, for grass or trees or flowers planted in straight, distinct rows. But my vision was blurred by quick bursts of movement, small streaks of activity flashing by, unwilling to slow down even for a second and announce themselves.

"Dogs," I observed.

With the next step Amnon and I were separated, as the scripts of our lives demanded. Dodging Frisbees and balls, I watched my first love rush headlong into the canine traffic, seeking camaraderie through collision, escape through entanglement, in various hues of brown. By the time I caught up with him he was fully transformed, his face licked clean and luminous, his clothing muddied and covered with hair. And he was ready to introduce me.

"Nava, meet Aviram and Hadar. And over there are Rafaela and Paili, and look, here comes Yarkona, always the center of attention. Shalom, Yarkona!"

The dogs were mostly small, reflecting the size of the country they lived in. Small and suffused with an unquenchable spirit, like the Zionist forebears of their owners, and of Amnon. I thought that maybe if I smiled, he would realize how serious the situation was.

"Yarkona?" I grinned, shielding my face from an inquisitive snout. "Isn't that the name of a park?"

Amnon returned my smile, happy to see me so engaged. Or, more likely, it was Yarkona he was smiling at. "The Yarkon Park, yes, it's on the other side of the city. 'Yarkona' comes from *yarok*, which as you know means 'green.' I can take you there tomorrow."

Tomorrow was fine, but we were still in the throes of today. "Where are all the people?" I wanted to know. I tried to look up, but Yarkona kept matching my movements with spastic ones of her own, as if trying to convey an important tiding that, unlike the park that shared her name, could not wait until tomorrow.

"Nava, meet Ayelet, a person."

With his confident hands, Amnon conjured up a woman standing before us, black-eyed and beautiful, an unclaimed leash latched to her wrist.

"Nava?" she repeated. "You are Israeli?"

She asked this question as if we were back on the kibbutz again, as if this were the beginning, and not the end.

"I'm just here to see Amnon," I explained. "Just for a few days."

Ayelet shrugged and began to separate the thick cords of her hair into three parts. "*Vat-ever,*" she said, the *r* rising directly from her throat. She started to braid.

This calmness amidst the chaos, I could not accept it. It made me want to scream and run rabidly around in circles. It made me want to fall to the ground and stir more dirt into the park stew.

Yarkona saw the saliva form at the corners of my mouth and took it as a cue to nip at my heels. I shook her off. "Your dog wants to play," I lied to Ayelet, who was still braiding away.

"She likes you," Ayelet lied back to me, or maybe it was the truth. It didn't matter.

"She's a sweet dog," I said.

I shook Yarkona off again.

The sky was darkening now, the streetlights snapping on and restoring a semblance of order to a city that eschewed all rules. "Where are all the *other* people?" I tugged at Amnon's sleeve, trying to break the spell that he had cast upon himself. Perhaps they were already gone, and the beasts had taken over.

Extending his arm into the air, Amnon caught a Frisbee, then flung it back in the direction from which it had come. "Relax," he said, slightly out of breath. "You're in Israel now."

On the way home we walked side by side, our steps synchronized but set into motion by thoughts that had nothing in common. As if to compensate for the trauma unfolding, colors bloomed around us as we walked: pink bougainvillea cascading along stone ledges, yellow cornflowers emerging from the cracks in the sidewalk, potted marigolds perched outside high windows. And the street signs: Bialik, Trumpeldor, Tchernichovsky, all swathed in the green I missed from home.

At Rothschild Boulevard, I left the ground behind and stretched my body toward the trees, lone oaks planted a century before in the sand. Then I steered Amnon to the bench from earlier and sat him down. "If they kill Hebrew like they killed Yiddish, I'll still have my name," I reasoned, trying to sort things out while there was still time. "Maybe that's why my parents gave it to me."

There was room for four people on the bench, and Amnon filled nearly every inch of it, shifting his body impatiently with each word that I directed his way. I knew it was a challenge for him to listen to me, just as it would be hard for me later, back at his apartment, to dream about our kibbutz days and not try to recreate them.

"Amnon, did you hear what I said?"

Amnon squirmed like a caterpillar emerging from his cocoon, ready to be reborn and take wing. At least, that was how I saw it.

And then, gradually, everything fell deathly silent: the vehicles in the streets and the drivers trying to force them through; the open-windowed conversations between neighbors; the broken piano, the piano teacher, the music sending out its supplications from Rabin Square. Even the dogs were gone. A moment before, I'd still been able to hear them, or if not them, others like them, barking at will. A moment before, I'd thought they would echo in my ears forever.

"Amnon, what's happening?"

At this question, Amnon stopped squirming and turned completely around on the bench, facing the back with his arms folded in front of him. "It looks like we're the only ones left," he said, staring into the darkness. "Maybe you were right after all."

For several more minutes the city remained frozen in time, a held breath, an idea interrupted. And then, suddenly, a few streets over, the sea parted and the people came pouring out, first only a trickle, then a stream, and finally a wave of people welling up and washing over the city in search of dry land. I found myself leaning against Amnon.

"What happened, Amnon?"

He laughed, cradling my head in the crook of his arm, where it had positioned itself during the parting. "It's the middle of the night in America," he said, pointing to his watch. "Nothing happened, you fell asleep, took a little *shluf.* Sorry, but that's the only Yiddish I know."

And then, without warning, Amnon reached for my hand, as if anticipating the old age that would come to him if he agreed to leave the country. "I know you want to stay," he said, meeting my eyes for the first time since my arrival. It was a bad time to have chosen to cry. "I knew it then, and I know it now. It's all right, Nava, you don't have to be afraid."

We sat there for a long time like that, holding hands in a half sleep, under the trees.

Daughters of Respectable Houses

I'm not sure why I spotted Sophie's coat before I spotted Sophie, since her coat was arguably the least compelling thing about her. It was long and black and should have been made of leather; that's probably why it commanded so much attention. It should have been leather, but it wasn't. Not even faux leather. It was the kind of coat you had to touch to believe how poorly made it was—a plastic of such a low grade as to be immune to the economics of recycling. Whenever Sophie's coat came into view from the top of the street, I was sure it had grown a second skin to keep away the elements; but before I could touch it to see, she would lean forward to plant a kiss on each of my cheeks, then plunge her hands into her pockets as a prelude to complaining about how cold she was. She was always complaining about the cold.

She was in town for only a semester, and I was in no rush to befriend her. I had plenty of friends, a husband, and three children who hung at my neck and demanded kisses every evening before bedtime, even though they were boys. It was remarkable, really; I wasn't lacking a thing in the world.

It was my husband, as head of the history department, who had plucked Sophie from a pile of applicants to join the faculty as a scholar-in-residence. On the night of her arrival he arranged a dinner that I attended to help make conversation—and, more importantly, to help facilitate conversation between Sophie and Daniel, a colleague I had identified as being a perfect match for Sophie even before meeting her. Setting people up is always fun, even if you don't have the best track record. A few minutes before we headed out, Daniel called to announce that he was coughing up phlegm the size of *umeboshi* plums and would not be able to join us. It was just me, Gabriel, and Sophie now. I grumbled all the way up the street.

She was supposed to be waiting at the front entrance of her building, which was dark and unfriendly and looked like a place where no one had ever waited for anyone before.

"You stay there, and I'll check the back," Gabriel offered, disappearing around the corner. Within seconds he had returned with Sophie, towering over the two of us in her long black coat and laughing at the mix-up as if she had not found an occasion to laugh in a long time. "I didn't even know there were two entrances," she said, laughing away. "I'm used to only one."

Sophie was hungry; at the restaurant, the food disappeared down her throat the moment it reached the table. While she ate she talked, nonstop, which I had not been prepared for, seeing that it was my role to keep the conversation going. After a few minutes I decided I would not participate in it or, if I could help it, in any future conversations like it; that's how superfluous I felt. And Gabriel—equally superfluous—didn't blame me. "All the stories I heard tonight I already heard on the drive back from the airport," he informed me on the way home. "Sorry, I should have warned you."

In bed, I remembered Daniel. "Should I pursue this match or not?" I asked my husband. We lay stretched out like two corpses, exhausted from an evening in which we had hardly uttered a word.

Even though Gabriel had previously approved of my plan, he seemed surprised by the question. "Didn't you notice Sophie's hair, and the way she dresses, and the size of her hands?" he asked.

"Not really," I admitted. "Do you think leather coats in California are hard to come by?" Maybe she couldn't afford one, or hadn't expected winters where we lived to be so cold.

"She's obviously a lesbian," he said. "So save Daniel for someone else."

My husband always figures things out before I do; maybe that's why he's a professor while I tutor twelve-year-old boys for their bar mitzvahs. All that's required of me is that I carry a tune.

"You're right, of course she is," I agreed. I summoned up her short, spiky hair and huge hands. "And wasn't she wearing an oversized blazer under her coat?" I could see it now, and the baggy gray sweater beneath that. She could have done a lot better for herself, even as a lesbian.

On days when I didn't tutor I stayed in bed, propped up against pillows, reading novels. I read from the moment Gabriel took the kids to school in the morning to the moment he returned with them in the afternoon, taking short breaks every hour or so to check e-mail, make a quick meal, or drag the vacuum cleaner perfunctorily across whatever floor needed it the most, usually the kitchen, since between my quick meals I liked to snack, and not always sitting down or over a plate.

I'm not sure why my husband let me lie in bed all day—maybe because he loved me? Or because he knew that it was safer for me to live in Isaac Bashevis Singer's 1920s Warsaw or Jane Austen's Pemberley than in dinky Lorraine? Whatever the reason, I was grateful he held no grudges, even when dinner was not always ready for him at the end of a hard day's work. My kids must have thought I was a very busy woman up there in my room with the door closed.

The minute Daniel was over his flu, he made reservations at Al Hamra, then called to invite me along. "With Sophie, of course," he added, in case I didn't get the picture. "And Gabriel." Daniel's charm broke out only in the presence of multiple bodies. When he hung out with Gabriel, he only talked about grants that would get him out of Lorraine.

I should have told him to forget about it, that while Sophie cultivated many interests, men were not one of them. Instead I told my husband to call a babysitter, and off we went.

The restaurant was Moroccan, which for most people in Lorraine evoked no association of any kind; the place was usually empty. Sophie was wearing her big blazer again, a long, billowy skirt that hid every inch of her legs, and John Lennon eyeglasses that were crying out to be traded in for contact lenses. Daniel took one look at her, then spent the entire evening talking to Gabriel.

I ordered first, four small dishes: eggplant, butternut squash with cilantro, grilled peppers, and that chicken-filled pastry whose name I always forget, with the cinnamon and powdered sugar sprinkled on top.

The waitress wrote down my order and then turned to Sophie, whose eyes had enlarged to twice their normal size—and they were big to begin with. "I was going to order exactly the same things!" she revealed to everyone at the table, just like that, with an audible exclamation point at the end. Transmitting her elation by means of a set of impressively straight teeth, she regarded me as if I were the special of the day, newly unveiled. "Cilantro lovers always find each other," she said, in an undertone now, which was far worse than the exclamation point. "I grow it in pots on my balcony back home."

Until that moment, I hadn't been aware that I harbored any unconscious prejudices against lesbians. Together with Gabriel, I have always been a live-and-let-live kind of person, and I figured that as long as I didn't need to share my meal with her, Sophie was just fine the way she was. But when she assigned me the title of *lover*—never mind that it was in reference to an herb—I was forced to consider, for those few seconds, the blue eyes blinking behind those awful glasses, and it was all I could do not to excuse myself from the table and get a breath of fresh air.

Later that night, I berated my husband for not letting me flirt with Daniel at the restaurant.

"Flirt with Daniel?"

"You know what I mean—just as a gesture, to apologize

for Sophie." I flexed my foot and felt my last few sips of wine flow into it.

Gabriel knew what I meant. He liked to flirt too, just enough to keep a small cosmopolitan spirit alive in Lorraine, and to stay off antidepressants.

"She was all over you, wasn't she."

It was neither a question nor a statement of truth. "Oh, come on, we talked about headaches the whole time." Headaches and cilantro. She couldn't understand why I tired of my squash after two bites, but was more than happy to relieve me of it.

"She gets them too?"

"Worse than me."

"Interesting."

It wasn't interesting at all, so I took off my shirt, then reached over and took off Gabriel's. Out of all our friends, Gabriel and I were the only ones who could have made a career out of our sex life. It wasn't just good; it was great.

For the next forty-five minutes, we changed the subject.

*

Warsaw, 1918. With the Russians out and the Germans on their way in, Singer's Jews were convinced that better times were just around the corner, and so was I, even though I knew what was coming and could not read more than a chapter at a time without getting palpitations and biting my lip.

I stayed there—with the door closed and the kids

playing on the other side of it—for the next several days. When the phone rang, I let it ring. When hunger called, I made a sandwich and brought it to bed, violating the strictest rule in the house and leaving trails of crumbs everywhere as evidence of my crime. In my sleep I saw young Asa Heshel on the front lines, with his bayonet and leaky boots, pining away for Hadassah; I saw Hadassah taking the waters in the countryside, in heat over Asa Heshel; Abram smoking a cigar on Krochmalna Street; Koppel closing the books on a family inheritance; Adele and Meshulam; Nyunie and Fishel; Rosa Frumetl, Gina, Leah—and the rabbis; let's not forget them: the Bialodrevna and the Novominsker, the Amshinover and the Kozhenitzer, all fighting like cats and dogs, heirs to competing dynasties destined to go under, to be snuffed out with a shot to the head or a single stream of gas. Those seven days were like a shivah for me that I marked not by sitting on a low stool and covering the mirrors, but by ordering takeout and letting dust accumulate in every corner of the house. If the cast of characters had been able to stand up and take a bow at the end of the book, the week would have been much easier for all of us to get through—not just for me, but for everyone in my family, who knew to stay away from me whenever I had the book in my hand. It was the double dying that made it so hard, the fiction interchangeable with the fact.

On the eighth day, my husband came home from work and said, "Sophie wants to go out for a drink."

My husband deserved a drink after all the housework I had heaped on him that week. I dare say he might have even been in serious need of one. "That's fine, I'll put the kids to bed tonight," I offered, happy to have an opportunity to help out while I was between books. I was a good mother, but I could have been better.

"No, with you," Gabriel clarified. "She wants to go out for a drink with you."

"With me?"

"She asked for your number."

My face flushed, as if attacked by an unknown allergen. I didn't like the way my husband was speaking to me at that moment, not at all. "Last time I checked, it was *our* number," I said, vaguely recalling that the phone had rung repeatedly during the last few chapters of Singer's book.

"You should go," Gabriel said. He was standing by the refrigerator now, peering inside at its emptiness. "I've had two lunch meetings with her now, and she's really not so bad."

*

It was raining when I arrived at the back entrance to Sophie's building, raining and freezing cold. Per Sophie's instructions, I pulled firmly at the door, which she had promised would be open. It was locked, and rain is never kind to people with curly hair, umbrella or no umbrella. I had forgotten mine. By the time Sophie appeared in the lobby, ten minutes late, my face had already been pressed against the glass door for five.

"Oh, you poor thing! It's freezing out here!"

Outside, Sophie took stock of the situation by

crossing her arms and rubbing them vigorously. She reached for the top button of her coat, then slipped it skillfully through its black plastic loop. A second later, I saw it slide out again.

I was a fast walker, but Sophie was an even faster one; it took us less than five minutes to reach the wine bar. At first I thought it was closed and, for the second time that evening, found my face pressed against glass. Through my cupped hands I could make out flickering candles and a flurry of activity from a single table in the corner. "It's pretty empty in there," I said. "Should we try somewhere else?"

Sophie opened the door and marched right in. "I don't mind if I'm the only person in a restaurant," she said. "Oh, look who's here!"

Sitting at the table in the corner was my husband's (and now Sophie's) colleague, Seth Eisenberg. Across from him sat a man I didn't recognize, handsomely dressed in the requisite sports jacket over a black T-shirt, and already extending his hand for an introduction. I watched Sophie shake it and say, "Sophie."

"Sofia?"

"Sophie," she repeated, and didn't seem happy about it.

"Oh, I'm sorry. A wise name either way."

Sophie turned to Seth. "And how are you?"

"Not bad," Seth replied. But before I could join in and ask why not good, Sophie was already out the door.

Back in the rain, the first thing she did was take her scarf and tie it around her head like a babushka, having, like me, forgotten her umbrella. Or maybe she preferred the looks from passersby that this elicited, Lorraine being a good five thousand flight miles from Saint Petersburg.

"Have you ever seen such a snake?" Sophie turned to me and smiled that big smile of hers, happy that it was just the two of us again.

I didn't have the faintest idea what she was talking about. "Seth?" I asked. I rather liked him, though I preferred him with a beard. Tonight he'd been clean-shaven.

"Not Eisenberg. The other guy." Sophie *tsk*ed at me for not seeing the obvious. "What a snake. Ick. Eisenberg should pick better drinking partners."

With that clarification, I still had no idea what she was talking about. I was not the kind of person who believed that lesbians hated all men. Or even most men. I understood that they simply loved women.

"Why do you call him Eisenberg?" I asked.

Sophie smiled. "As a tribute to Yaakov Shabtai," she said dreamily.

"The author?" I can still quote the opening of *Past Continuous* from memory: *Goldman's father died on the first of April, whereas Goldman himself committed suicide on the first of January. . . .*

"He called his characters by their last names."

"Goldman," I nearly whispered.

"MY GOD!" Sophie shouted her praise like an evangelist. "We are like two drops of water, you and I."

By the time we'd hung up our coats and paper towel–dried our hair, two seats had freed up at the bar, which we grabbed as if our lives depended on it. The dining area was packed, and a line was starting to form out the door.

I was planning to order a glass of wine, but Sophie studied the cocktail menu with great interest. "I want to order something quintessentially Southern while I'm in the South," she announced, underlining each offering with her finger. "Maybe the Lemondrop Martini, or Bob's Island Special? As long as it doesn't have any artificial cherries in it. They give me an instant migraine."

The bartender was standing in front of us, eavesdropping. I wondered what made us interesting enough for him to do that and hoped he wasn't jumping to any small-town conclusions about Sophie and me. My wedding band was on the thin side, but not invisible.

"I would definitely go with the mojito," he suggested, taking down a clean glass and giving it a spin. "It's got some lime juice in it, rum, mint, sugar, and a splash of seltzer. Classic American drink."

"From Cuba," I added.

Eyes twinkling, Sophie closed the menu. I don't think she had ever had a cocktail of any kind before, and she looked very excited. Then again, that's pretty much how she always looked. "I'll take it," she said.

While Sophie was talking about her grandfather's Florida factory and every component of the electric wheelchairs it had developed over the last decade to international acclaim, I couldn't help wondering whether going out for a drink with an unattached lesbian was akin to consorting with an unmarried man, and, if so, why my husband was so keen on my doing it. Shouldn't he have swept me into his arms and insisted I stay home? Warned me to be careful? Suggested dessert instead of a drink? Gabriel knows that it takes only half a glass of wine before I start punctuating my conversation with frequent slaps to the knee of whoever is at the receiving end of it. Tonight it was Sophie.

"So when the Chinese asked every country participating in the Olympics to send them the name of its national flower and bird," Sophie was saying, "Israel realized it was high time to come up with one."

"Israel didn't have a national flower or bird until now?"

"Until now," she confirmed. Then she laughed and took another sip of her mojito.

My wineglass was half-empty, but I tried to keep my hands to myself. My head was spinning with curiosity. "So what are they?"

Sophie leaned forward. "First let me tell you what they aren't. The Israeli national bird is not the griffon vulture, even though it is quite prominent in the north, near Mount Carmel."

"Too violent?"

"Too violent. And endangered in the rest of the country, which is not the kind of symbol Israel wants to promote."

She continued. "And it's also not the bulbul, though this was the first choice of many Israelis, who saw in the bird a mirror image of themselves: loud and obnoxious—and a loyal friend to the end. But *bulbul* is children's slang for penis, so that was out too." Sophie laughed again, and this time I joined in.

I had not expected a penis, in any context, to enter

into the evening's conversation, and the bar stools we occupied were swivel ones. When the wine in me sent my hand toward Sophie's knee, my stool spun out of control, and I nearly ended up in her lap. That is, both my hands landed on both of her knees.

"Whoa! Sorry about that. Did you say *penis*?" And what's more, without blushing, as if she was comfortable with the concept.

Sophie didn't smooth out the creases in her pants that my hands had made. She left them right where they were. "In the end, 150,000 people voted for the *duchifat*—the hoopoe bird in English." She described it to me in detail, without taking her eyes off me for a second. "In Leviticus, the *duchifat* is described as unclean and forbidden food, which means the Israeli national bird isn't kosher!"

For the next several minutes we bantered like this, encouraged by the competing stimuli around us, and of course the wine and mojito. It was only when we ordered a second round that things got complicated.

I didn't have any illusions about Sophie's literary preferences; as a historian who specialized in modern Israel, she couldn't be expected to have a soft spot for Isaac Bashevis Singer, or for Yiddish novels in general. So when I confided to her, with alcohol-induced tears in my eyes, that I was living in two parallel worlds, one of which no longer existed, it came as quite a shock to see tears gathering in her eyes as well. And that she wasn't wearing her glasses.

"*The Family Moskat*?" she asked. "Is that the book you're talking about?"

"Why, do you know it?"

"Know it?" She *tsk*ed at me again. "*The Family Moskat* is the only six-hundred-page book I've ever read twice. It's been in my blood for years."

We were both more than a little tipsy now, but that wasn't enough to account for the adrenaline coursing through my veins, or the fact that for the first time that evening I felt conscious of how I looked.

For the next hour we didn't just talk about Singer and *The Family Moskat*; we relived every one of its six hundred pages. And while we talked, we got hungry and ordered food, first a plate of polenta fries, then a dish of asparagus, and finally the $25 steak special, which we took turns eating with one fork, even though the server had brought us two.

"What about Abram's love for Hadassah?" I asked when I could eat no more. In my drunken state I planted my eyes on Sophie and kept them there; without her glasses covering them up her irises were a dazzling blue, like the Warsaw summer sky.

Sophie noticed me staring, and smiled. "What about it?"

I shifted my gaze to her teeth. "Do you think it was merely platonic?"

"What, do you really think there's such a thing as platonic love?"

"I don't know, do you?"

"I don't believe that love can transcend mortal life, or that it is a gift from the gods, no," Sophie said. "Abram lusted after Hadassah like the lecher he was. I wouldn't try to interpret his behavior any other way."

At that moment I excused myself to go to the bathroom. It was either that or risk another fall from my swivel chair, the temptation of which was suddenly very strong. My hands were trembling as I got up.

In the bathroom, I turned my spinning head upside down to refresh my curls. Then I peed, readjusted my outfit and necklace, washed my hands, and reapplied my lipstick.

It took me a long time to return to the bar; I kept bumping into things, and everybody observing me looked so sympathetic, I had to smile to let them know how sweet they were. When I finally found my way back to Sophie, something was not right; she was not there. Or rather, she was there, but not alone. In my chair sat a tall, dark figure that, as I approached, I was able to identify as Eisenberg, and next to him, standing as close to Sophie as possible without merging with her entirely, the snake.

"Well, hello, gentlemen," I greeted them, emphasizing *men* as I glanced at Sophie.

But Sophie made no effort to separate herself from the snake, even as he closed in to examine the watch on her wrist and announce with a childish grin, "Friends, the night is still young!" From the lustful look in her eyes, she didn't seem to mind his hiss at all.

In my desperation I tried to take refuge in Eisenberg, chatting him up like the good wife of his colleague that I was. I even offered to buy him a drink on the condition that he would pay for all the drinks and food I had ordered from his chair. With a single jump he gave it back to me, but it did not bring me closer to Sophie.

She had already spread her blue eyes so thin, there was no Warsaw sky left for me to consider anymore.

The check arrived and while we paid, the snake kept on hissing. "Oxo felt so empty after you ladies left that I declared the night couldn't end until we found you. And voilà! Here you are!"

Sophie really liked that exclamation point. "Here I am!" she confirmed, though the *you* had clearly been used in the plural.

*

After Sophie left with the snake that night, Eisenberg had no choice but to walk me home; Gabriel would have heard all about it if he hadn't. It was still raining, and as he shook out his wet coat he offered to share his umbrella with me, a red-and-white monster of a thing with the words "INDIANA HOOSIERS" written on it. I didn't ask for an explanation.

"Thanks, Eisenberg," I said, and stepped under the canopy.

"Eisenberg? Where did that come from?" he asked, as though he had never heard his own name before.

It was a legitimate question, but now that Sophie was gone I wasn't about to give her any credit for the answer. "Yaakov Shabtai," I said, shrugging. "An Israeli writer who died of a heart attack at the age of forty."

We said good-bye outside my house. "Thanks for seeing me home," I said, forcing a smile when I would have preferred to throw up. I could also detect the first signs of a migraine coming on.

"No problem." He gave me a little half bow before reclaiming his umbrella. Then he handed me the coat he had shaken out but not put on.

"Wait, don't forget this," he said, handing me not his coat and not my coat but Sophie's, all nine yards of it. "The bartender gave it to me on the way out."

Sophie's coat. I could have taken it from him and given it to Sophie. Or given it to Gabriel to give to Sophie. Or simply kept it for myself as a memento, or as something to burn the next time we made a fire. But no, I didn't hate Sophie, not at all. I only understood that it was men she loved, and not me.

"Actually, that's not my coat," I said, stepping back a few feet to avoid contact with it. "But it was nice of you to carry it. Is it waterproof?"

Shaking his head, Seth slung the coat over his shoulder like a locker room towel. "Hardly. It weighs a ton from all the water in it." He rotated his shoulder toward me. "Here, feel."

"That's OK, I believe you."

It was the last I saw of that coat, which Sophie had shed the next time I saw her, like the second skin I had somehow expected it to grow. We were headed in the same direction when we ran into each other a week after the wine bar, but even after she kissed me on the cheek I couldn't bring myself to ask where she was going. And a week after that, when she called to propose another evening out, I was too engrossed in a second round with my Singer book to accept her invitation.

Contamination

Igor spends most of his mornings in a cave, across the street from the park where we used to grill hamburgers and toss Frisbees over each other's heads. While I sit in my office filing papers and answering phone calls, he crouches quietly on a cold limestone surface under the ground, scraping mineral deposits into a brown leather pouch.

Today, when we meet for lunch, bits of gray sediment fall from his hair onto the table. Igor brushes them off and asks me how my morning was. I observe in him a man trying to understand the structure and processes of the earth, and find his question impossible to answer. I think of gypsum crystals, saltpeter, the skeletons of animals thousands of years old buried in the cavern fills above Igor's head. Looking down, I reply, "No, how was *your* morning?"

After lunch I return to my office and study the people around me. Some I can smell but not see; others I can see but not hear. Russel approaches my desk and hands me a slip of paper with the letters *k-r-u-m-h-o-l-z* written on it. "You think that's right?" he asks shyly. "It's not a name you come across every day."

I examine the letters and with a red pencil change the *u* to an *o* and insert a *t* before the *z*. "I know this man," I say. "Business-process reengineering. Quality-management facilitation. You'll have to do more to get on his good side than spell his name right."

Russel nods and backs away. "I hear he's tough as nails. But his wife does spectacular flower arrangements for wedding receptions. Some catering too. Ed thinks we shouldn't write her off."

I go home with a bag of groceries and a headache. Igor is sitting at the kitchen table, legs crossed, reading a book. I ask him if he wants a turkey sandwich for dinner, and he shakes his head. I ask him if he wants a baked potato with sour cream, and he shakes his head again. I peer into the grocery bag and empty what's left, a carton of eggs and an overripe avocado. "If possible, I'd like the carton of eggs," Igor requests. "But if possible, just the carton."

While I make myself an omelet, Igor spoons out mineral samples from various containers into each compartment of the egg carton. "Bat droppings," he announces with the third spoonful. "Try to guess why they are black."

I guess: "From the bats." I guess: "From the darkness of the cave."

Igor holds up the spoon, and I cover my plate with my hand. "From the horny shells of insects that bats eat, but can't digest," he explains. "They're rich in phosphorous and other substances that can be used as fertilizer."

As Igor fills the compartments, arranging his data for preservation and future reference, I think of the filing I do in the office. Unlike my work, Igor's data, once stored away, has the ability to change form, or to decompose and disappear entirely, leaving behind nothing but a pungent odor or a faint suggestion of what it once was. I offer him a final forkful of omelet, which he rejects, and leave the plate in the sink.

After dinner, Igor laments the conditions in which he is compelled to work. "Every morning I have to wait in line with the tourists until a man in a flannel shirt comes and unlocks the gate barring the entrance to the cave. Once inside, I take refuge in a narrow slot that connects a dome pit with an older main passage. There I can hope for five minutes of solitude during which I collect the samples I need and explore the area undisturbed. After those five minutes, when my speleologist work ceases, I become indistinguishable from the hordes of people making their way toward me, squealing at a small crustacean or lining up to take a picture of a calcite rod."

Igor knows he is not a speleologist, but an immigrant from Russia with an interest in anything that does not require him to sit at a desk. When one passion wanes, another takes its place. I have renewed my promise—after breaking it in an episode with birds—to support him in his pursuits, and not to interfere.

I ask Igor why he needs solitude to collect mineral samples. Before answering, he closes the egg carton and puts it in the refrigerator. "Solitude prevents contamination," he says simply. While I wait for him to explain, he walks into the living room and turns on the television. From the kitchen I hear the voices of contestants and the countdown of a clock. I imagine myself sitting next to Igor on the couch, hearing the same sounds, seeing the same images. I remain in the kitchen and pick at a scab on my knee, the only activity I can conceive of that's comparable to the one taking place in the other room. We spend the rest of the evening apart, like cave spores, settling into separate environments to germinate and develop—in the best of all possible outcomes—into a mature form of the species.

The next morning I arrive at work an hour early. In the darkness of my cubicle I file a stack of papers, write a memo, pour myself a cup of coffee. When these tasks are complete, I run my hands along the panels of the cubicle and feel for what I know is not there—a secret passage, a narrow slot that opens up to a crawl space padded with the last five hundred letters I have had to answer. My fingers wander over the top of the highest panel to explore a side known to me by sight but not by touch. My body leans heavily against the plastic, allowing my fingers more room to maneuver. When they can reach no higher, a foreign, sweaty hand clamps down on them, and I scream.

Russel's head peers over the divider, a dark sun rising from the west. "That was fun," he says eagerly, letting go of my hand. "Kind of like a pantomime, or Morse code, but with an element of the workaday world thrown in. What were you trying to signal?"

I turn my back to Russel, facing the identical panel on the other side. "Why are you sitting at your desk in the dark?"

"I got here early to type up a letter to Kromholtz," he says. "It reminded me of the late-night movies I used to watch when I couldn't fall asleep. One actually took place in an office building, pretty high up too, just like this one. Maybe you saw it, something with *hemlock* in the title?"

Igor and I never have trouble falling asleep. Sometimes, when our eyes have already committed themselves to unconsciousness, our hands wander languidly across the sheets until they come to rest on a shoulder or a half-exposed breast. It is as close as we come to intimacy these days; if we are lucky, dreams complete the gesture and bring us a little closer.

I walk over to the door and turn on the lights. "Finish your letter to Kromholtz," I advise Russel. "Forget about the hemlock movie."

Russel returns to his desk, alternately nodding and shaking his head. "You probably think the hemlock was in the coffee, but it wasn't. It was in the bathroom soap. Went right through the skin. The killer wanted to see who washed their hands after using the toilet and who didn't. Those who didn't suffered a worse fate than the others. You don't want to know."

It is barely eleven thirty when Igor appears at my cubicle, accompanied by a young man in a thick flannel shirt and hiking boots. Igor is visibly nervous; he too is dressed in flannel—a shirt I have never seen before, nearly identical to the young man's—and makes no attempt to wipe his blackened hands before reaching for mine and leading me out the door.

"This is Tom," he says, introducing the young man as we step into the elevator. "The cave warden."

Tom chuckles and begins to fiddle with what looks like the head of a small, high-powered flashlight in his breast pocket. "Igor is always the first one to arrive in the morning, trying to beat the crowds," he says. "Sometimes I wish I could just hand him the keys and go back to bed."

Igor squeezes my hand, and I feel the grime of ten thousand years enter my bloodstream. "Are we going to the cave now?" I ask, confused.

Outside, he lets go of my hand and picks up his pace, leaving Tom and me to follow. "Of course not," he calls out over his shoulder. "The cave is closed for lunch, so I thought we could eat together. It opens again in one hour, so we have to hurry."

Within three minutes, Tom, Igor, and I are sitting at a plastic table in the McDonald's around the corner. The restaurant is full, and the smell of disinfectant strong. I feel that if I crane my neck just enough, I will be able to peer out the door and around the corner and spot Russel, his face pressed against the office window seven stories up, his hands pantomiming indistinct but fateful signals in my direction.

Before any of us gets up to place an order, Igor slaps a hand against his forehead, a gesture he's learned since coming to America but has not yet mastered, and hurriedly excuses himself to retrieve a brown bag lunch he claims to have left in my office. "The sardines only had one more day," he explains to Tom. "And today was the day."

Hamburgers in hand, Tom and I wait passively for Igor to return. Tom asks me about work, and I ask Tom about Igor. Among other things, I want to know how Igor conducts himself in the presence of others in the cave, whether in the process of collecting his mineral samples he scorns the tourists who get in his way or treats them with respect. I do not tell Tom why such information is of interest to me, that it will help me calculate, when Igor sits at the kitchen table separating his findings into the good and the bad, just how far the contamination has spread.

Tom does not know the answers to my questions, but explains that occasional short-temperedness is common in low-pressure cave environments. “I’ve been known to lose it a few times myself,” he assures me. “Usually in the dark zone, where the beetles and the bats are. They still freak me out, even after all my training.”

I nod and take another bite of my hamburger. I feel that if I crane my neck just enough, I will be able to peer out the door and see Igor running full speed in the direction of the cave, then stopping to hail the cab that will whisk him to his destination. Once he has arrived, he will try to jump the fence—once, twice—that separates him from the solitude he has been seeking. On the third try, just when Tom and I have reached for the French fries at the same time and grazed the tips of each other’s fingers, he will succeed.

Invasions

What I thought I wanted to do was move to Paris. Or Rome. Or Tel Aviv. Stinkbugs fell from the ceiling onto my head while I slept, and the Food Lion in town was forever out of vegetables. But that's not why I left Ohio. I left Ohio because a man lived there who loved me.

He would have been waiting for me with a three-course meal every evening when I came home from work, only I didn't have a job, so I was the one waiting for him, and I didn't know how to cook. We ate variations of pasta until neither of us could fit into our pants anymore; then we switched to rice and got even bigger. BJ joined Gold's Gym while I excreted calories at home, reading novels that made me cry and shifting with the sun like the hands of a very slow clock.

We knew our neighbors from the recyclables they left out on the curb every Friday morning. Most were beverage containers: sodas and juices and cheap beers whose smell followed you as you walked up the street. In the paper bins were pizza boxes and newspapers—many still rolled up and rubber-banded—and an occasional assemblage of cardboard flaps that had recently housed a television or piece of faux-wood furniture from Walmart. When the garbage truck came rattling along, I stopped whatever I was doing and listened to the squeak of the tires and the heave-ho of another seven days of crap being hauled away. Sometimes I went outside and kicked the bins into their proper places at the top of the driveway, but usually I left them on the sidewalk for BJ. I wanted their lightness to give him pause.

One Friday morning shortly before the garbage truck made its rounds, I took a walk around the block. Over the past week, I had begun to question my ritual of acknowledging the truck's arrival, my ears perking up as if by some atavistic pull. As I turned onto Dice Street, red bin after red bin met my every step. Their haphazard positions made it impossible for me to walk in a straight line, so I wove like a drunkard, in and out and sometimes over, until it started to feel like a game and I forced myself to stop. In two months I would turn thirty.

At the top of the street a cat jumped out of one of the bins and sent a wine bottle rolling toward me. It was the first wine bottle I had seen in the neighborhood, and it would not be the last—as I approached the bin, six additional bottles stretched their necks out.

I knew that if I lingered I would start wondering about this wine, who drank it and for what purpose and why wasn't I invited. I would stare at the small blue house on the corner until someone came out of it, or went into it, and wonder why I hadn't noticed him before and whether the wines—each hailing from a different French château—were a good enough reason to notice him now. I was sure it was a him, because the circumstances of my life demanded it. Even BJ would have had a hard time claiming otherwise, and he might not even have tried.

When BJ got home that night, I rested my head on his big belly and sighed. "Let's move to Bordeaux," I said, conjuring up a vineyard, the Eiffel Tower, and a slew of waiters named Pierre. "Let's move to Paris."

BJ chuckled, and my head bobbed up and down like a boat at sea. "Getting restless again?" he replied, combing his fingers through my hair. "A woman asked me for a prescription for Valium today. She said she's going on a trip, and is afraid of flying."

I waited for the punch line, but it didn't come. "And?"

"And I gave it to her."

BJ is a family doctor; my hair was full of the DNA of at least a dozen of his patients. "Why are you telling me this? Do you think I need Valium?" There was no hint of hostility in my voice—on the contrary, a good tranquilizer might have quashed my wanderlust for a few months, given me the state of mind conducive to sleeping ten hours straight with the TV and lights on.

"Not if I come with you," BJ said.

"Come with me where?"

"To Paris."

He loved me enough to give shape to my amorphous thoughts, even when I should have kept them to myself. I wasn't going to Paris, and BJ wasn't coming with me. The neighbor's house seemed so far away at that moment, I had to hug BJ hard to bring it into view. With each squeeze, I felt the time we had left together ticking away, the bed we were lying on lifting off the ground and getting ready to take off.

"Just print out one of my editing signs and put it up at work tomorrow, OK?" I said.

BJ was undressing now, misattributing the cri de coeur of my hugs and squeezes to a heightened sexual state. His clothes fell onto the floor in a heap, his belt lashing the rug like a whip in a circus.

"I'll do more than that," he replied. My breasts were in his hands, two firm models of cooperation and constancy. "I'll put up a dozen."

*

I was too old to gaze out the window for a glimpse of him, so I walked up onto his porch and knocked on his door. Of course no one was home; it was the middle of the day. But I had a book with me, and aside from some bird droppings and dried mud, the porch swing looked just fine. I settled in for a few chapters and waited.

It was a bad habit of my mother's to always send me old Yiddish novels in translation. She thought that if I spent enough time back in the shtetl, I would stop complaining about my life in Ohio and realize that scouring the Food Lion for organic broccoli was nothing compared to the forced conscription of ten-year-old Jewish boys into the tsarist army. She didn't understand that if the shtetl still existed, I would be on the first plane to Pinsk and would never come back.

I was so absorbed in the book that I didn't see him coming until his two leather-clad feet were directly in front of me. "Sholem Aleichem," he said, and pointed to my book.

It was a standard shtetl greeting, but we were in

Ohio, and not the Cleveland part; surely I had misheard. "Oh, sorry," I replied, and rose quickly to my feet. My rear end had disturbed the mud and bird shit from the swing, and perhaps he had liked them there. Plus I was, technically, trespassing.

He pointed to my book again. "You're reading Sholem Aleichem."

It was not a question, but it certainly begged one.

"You know Sholem Aleichem?" It was slightly embarrassing to pronounce the guttural *ch* of his name, even with it still hanging in the air, and for a moment I held the book aslant, as if my eyes had never shed a single tear onto its pages.

"Know him? I grew up on Sholem Aleichem."

At these words, I gave myself permission to study the mouth that had issued them, and to stop staring at his feet. I had seen that face before, in the neighborhood and around town, but had always taken it for Italian. He was as dark as any Jew whose ancestors had never intermarried could be, and BJ always joked that I was the last of those left. That's why he liked touching my hair so much.

"My mother started sending them when I moved here. I grew up on formula." Unflinching honesty was the bedrock of my relationship with BJ; I was beginning to anticipate a difficult conversation when he got home.

"Elliot." He put his briefcase down and held out his hand.

After a single pump, I let go. We were too good a fit. "Rona." I nodded. "I saw all those wine bottles in your garbage and—"

"The Merlots? I order them by the case; want to try one?"

"—I got curious."

I wasn't planning to cross the threshold, at least not that day; I was sure that more decisive words would come to me while he fumbled for his key. That the door was already unlocked I could not have foreseen, nor any of what happened when I followed Elliot inside his house. There are some experiences that are so regrettable, you want to repeat them just to marvel at all the missteps made along the way—and of course alter a few details afterward to completely undo them.

Elliot's house reminded me of my worst student days, when living with multiple roommates precluded any rules that would help ensure a semblance of sanity and decorum. Takeout containers from the cheapest restaurants in town covered nearly every available surface, while open books littered the remaining ones, their spines smashed into submission by several bulk-size containers of Ovaltine. In the kitchen alone three cats sauntered by, swishing their tails like broken windshield wipers and using my leg as a lint brush. Along the rail of a spiral staircase an assortment of socks was laid out to dry, together with several undershirts and a lone Fruit of the Loom; at the bottom of the staircase an empty laundry basket stood, begging to be filled.

Elliot observed me making mental notes of everything and smiled broadly when I ventured into the living room, rather than bolting out the front door. The windows were tall in this part of the house and the midday sun streamed through them, accentuating all the things I was hurrying to leave behind and introducing new ones, such as an exquisitely crafted floor-to-ceiling wine rack featuring art deco sunburst motifs and chevrons, its carved-out cubbies deep and inviting and totally empty.

Given the book that had gotten me into this, I saw no reason not to express my exasperation with a Yiddish favorite. "*Nu?*"

Elliot sanctioned my question with a vigorous nod; his eyebrows jumped to within an inch or two of his hairline. "Isn't it a beauty? I commissioned it from a carpenter friend before I learned the house had a cellar. It would make a great columbarium if I didn't have the cats." Stretching out his arm, he offered me his hand a second time. "Come on, let's take a bath."

*

It was with the idea of BJ, rather than BJ himself, that I first fell in love. I had been in Ohio for two weeks, copyediting in a cubicle with fluorescent lights that made for a near-constant migraine. After several concerned calls from my mother, I promised I would get myself to a doctor, or at least to a doctor's prescription. But when I inquired over the phone about a refill for Imitrex, I was told, in the bluntest of terms, that if I had just arrived from Chicago I would need to make a new patient appointment, and might have to wait several weeks to be seen. It took a lot of tears to get that woman to do her job. Dr. Middleton could see me on Friday, she finally said.

By Friday my migraine had passed, and I was so grateful to have my head back that I didn't even try to conceal my lust for BJ when he introduced himself, extending a freshly sanitized hand.

His belly protruded from beneath the white coat just enough to make me feel beautiful. I can't explain it. I shook his hand, but it had already been touched by so many others, I let go of it at once.

"Rona," I said. "Can you feel my appendix for a second?" Reflexively I reached for BJ's stomach and poked around, channeling my lust in the only way I knew how.

"Mine's doing just fine, thanks." He took me for a mild eccentric, maybe, but nothing more. In this small town, I wanted more. Arguably deserved more. "How about lying down and we'll take a look?"

I did as the doctor instructed. I lay down and lifted up my shirt and waited to be pronounced fit as a fiddle so that we could move on to my lower back and tender right shoulder.

"Does this hurt?"

"Actually, yes."

"And here?"

"A little."

BJ stopped prodding and motioned for me to sit up again. "Your appendix is fine, but it wouldn't hurt to add some fiber to your diet."

"Fiber?"

"You could start with raisin bran or oatmeal. What do you usually eat for breakfast?"

It was my fault for having taken things this far. Back home, the girls I had grown up with were married and breast-feeding; all I wanted was a man to make me feel happy I was still single.

"Are you telling me I'm constipated?" I had thought such a subject was discussed quietly, if at all, and only among family members. BJ didn't even bother to lower his voice.

"It depends on what you eat for breakfast," he said. "Let me guess. A bagel with cream cheese? Or maybe a croissant?"

I shrugged, shook my head, nodded. I was mortified.

BJ understood and stood closer so we could smell each other. "I'd start with raisin bran," he said. "OK?"

"OK," I sniffed. "Can you bring some over?"

There was a lengthy pause while my doctor considered my unprecedented proposal, my pheromones, and the messages mediated by my eyes. It was clear to both of us that another migraine was on its way, brilliant and blinding; I would wait for the cereal in bed, with the curtains drawn.

Finally he said, "Sure."

*

I took my clothes off and got into the bath. Elliot was already in it, his hairy chest heaving with pleasure at the lavender-scented bubbles proliferating in the water and the sight of my accommodating body making the first wave. With BJ's image flitting before my eyes, I submerged myself completely for several seconds, coming up only after telling myself that though the ritual waters of a mikvah were traditionally confined to a public bathhouse adjacent to a synagogue, taking a bath with Elliot might still qualify as an act of religious expression. The blackness of his eyes brought me back to where I wanted to be.

"Have you read Mendele Mocher Sforim?" I wiggled my toes in the water and grazed them against Elliot's neck.

"Of course. Love him. My God, your breasts."

I had hoped we would talk about literature a little longer. That was half the reason I had taken off my clothes. The other half, as I have already suggested, was pure physiognomy. I didn't want to have to fly home to Chicago every time I hankered after that face.

Chicago. I had to leave it in order to love it again. For months Asian carp were threatening to invade the Great Lakes through the ship canal, and nobody wanted to think about anything else. My father suffered chest pains when he walked along the water to work in the morning, and at synagogue my mother stopped eating gefilte fish. My brother, ten years my junior, had a new girlfriend and left his bedroom only twice a day. My own unhappiness was also attributed to the city's clogged waterways. "For fish the US Army sends out a red alert but in Israel a Scud missile only receives yellow," Meital complained from under my brother's blanket. "Everything will be OK, Rona. Not to worry. Just brush your hair."

"I'm not worried about fish," I tried to explain. "I could care less about the stupid fish."

Meital nodded. "Your heart is somewhere else, like the early *halutzim.* Go east, and you will find it."

She had far too many body piercings to mean Zion, but I asked anyway. "You think I should go to Israel?"

"To Zion, to Jerusalem," Meital said. "The spiritual center of the Jewish people. It is waiting for you."

I raised one unpierced eyebrow. "So why aren't you there?"

"Next week we go to Los Angeles for my cousin's wedding, and then to Las Vegas to play the machines," Meital replied. "Come over sometime, and I'll show you my dress."

*

"Do women here find you handsome or repulsive?" I asked Elliot. It wasn't a brazen question; Elliot knew how fleshy his eyelids and lips were, and how solid his sniffer. He had known, the second he saw me on his porch, that I didn't give a hoot about his wine hoard.

"You're the only woman here now," he replied, grabbing my nipple between his toes and giving it a workout. "So tell me."

I didn't feel the need to be in Paris or Rome or Tel Aviv just then. Somehow I was in all of those places at once. "Historic," I replied, squinting. It was hard to keep my eyes open when there was foot traffic in my erogenous zones. "Your face belongs in an archive."

"An archive," Elliot repeated. "Suits me."

For the next few minutes we flopped around in the water like two clumsy children, our extremities colliding with the sides of the bathtub at every turn. Elliot explored my body like a scientist, holding up my feet to the light before snacking on them, then plunging into the depths to retrieve the next specimen. As I had feared, we were a good fit; if the bathtub had been larger, and if the cats had not suddenly come in to offer their commentary, meowing in protest at my high-pitched entreaties for more, I am ashamed to say that I would have betrayed BJ with nothing less than full penetration.

"Let's go into the bedroom," Elliot panted, shooing away the cats with a spritz of water. His penis pointed the way as he stood up.

I stopped squinting and took a good look around me. Ohio was everywhere.

"Shit. I'm getting a migraine."

"A migraine? You can orgasm it away. I get them too, sometimes."

"Not like mine, you don't."

"*Maydele,*" Elliot pleaded.

I shook my head, and it rattled. "A terrible migraine. I have to go."

*

At home, I drew the blinds and lay in the dark, my bottle of Imitrex sitting untouched on the nightstand like an abandoned idol. The stinkbugs were back and plinking around the room, each plink a thunderclap to my skull. I welcomed the mounting pain as punishment for what had transpired but kept my eyes closed, knowing that opening them would mean throwing up on BJ's pillow. BJ was in the hospital cafeteria now, reading the newspaper and eating chicken noodle soup from a Styrofoam cup. He was programmed to do this, but my own movements were unpredictable and impossible to chart. The other day, weighing in at 120 pounds, I'd found myself in the Woman's section at Talbots, shopping for a tunic; my mother stopped me midsentence when I tried to tell her about it that evening. She warned me that if I kept it up, there would soon be no turning back, and told me that she had put another book in the mail.

I knew, from the Mormons who prowled the neighborhood, that suffering was a sign of God's love, and that lepers could not feel pain in the leprous parts of their bodies. It made me wonder what kind of punishment I was inflicting upon myself. Even the bed had been made before I crawled into it, BJ having freed it from a coterie of Entenmann's crumbs that had settled between the sheets. He would be home in a few hours. There was only one choice at my disposal now, more consequential than all the others combined: to take an Imitrex and look into the mirror.

I was fit as a fiddle when BJ walked into the bedroom, smelling of hand sanitizer.

"Tiger, tiger, burning bright, in the forests of the night. Is it over, or just starting?"

I stretched my limbs taut, then quickly retracted them at the thought that I might resemble one of Elliot's cats. "Over," I said, and felt my eyes well up again. "You can open the blinds."

But BJ kept them closed and lay down next to me. "Was it a bad one?" He rolled onto his side and perused me in the dark from a propped elbow.

"Bad." The mirror had revealed the same me, only tearstained. "Did you eat chicken soup today?"

"Chicken soup? Why do you ask?"

"If I got my mother's recipe and made you a pot every day, would you come home for lunch from now on?"

BJ kissed my cheek, as if I had already put on an apron. "You bet I would."

I closed my eyes again. My mother was a lousy cook, and my father an impatient man. Soup had never found a place in our family.

"Actually, there's no recipe now, but I'm sure there was one once, a few generations back. When everyone had carp swimming in their bathtubs, and stuff like that."

"Carp?"

"For gefilte fish."

"Not a very sanitary place to take a bath."

BJ always brought his work home with him; there was no way around it. "You know that I left Chicago because of fish," I stated flatly. "Carp, as a matter of fact. And now we are talking about fish, as if they've followed me all the way here."

A cat meowed outside, just as BJ started to undress me. I closed my eyes and willed a dream to come in which he figured prominently, standing at a busy intersection, directing traffic. I willed a tunnel to appear, and when it failed to, an empty roll of toilet paper. But BJ was the doctor; I had no idea what a womb actually looked like.

I said, "I had sex with the neighbor today." And still he let me sleep until morning.

The Next Vilonsky

The sidewalks of Tel Aviv are hospitable to everything but foot traffic. As Dr. Vilonsky dodged a network of leashes and several dogs attached to them, a five-shekel coin fell out of his breast pocket and into the outstretched hand of a beggar, who was bent over an open newspaper.

"*Todah,*" the beggar thanked him, and continued reading.

"Oh, I'm sorry, that coin was for my granddaughter," Vilonsky informed him, shaking his leg free of a stray cat that had rubbed up against it. "I need it back."

The beggar turned his palm over and released the five shekels, along with two ten-agorot coins, onto the sidewalk. "*B'vakasha,*" he said.

Vilonsky coughed from deep within his chest. He hadn't expected interest. Reaching into his pants pocket, he pulled out a twenty-shekel bill. "*B'vakasha* to you." The bill was crumpled and fell, rather than floated, into the beggar's hand. Still, Vilonsky saw it float.

"Why not for the girl?" asked the beggar.

"You let me worry about her," replied Vilonsky. He stepped over a discarded chest of drawers and went on his way.

Vilonsky's granddaughter loved poppy-seed cake. Given the range of patisseries in the city, Vilonsky found Hagar's preference unfortunate, an evolutionary throwback to ancestors neither known nor asked about. Hagar spurned forks; she took aim at the cake with bare fingers, unfazed by the black seeds that rooted themselves between her teeth and under her nails. The whole operation always lasted no more than a few minutes, precluding any possibility of conversation between grandfather and granddaughter. Sometimes a sigh would escape from his mouth.

"What's wrong, *Saba*?" she'd asked once.

"Oh, nothing, Hagar. An old man needs to sigh sometimes, that's all."

"You look like an old Jew when you do that."

"An old Jew?"

"Like a rabbi, I mean. From Jerusalem. They always hum when they walk down the street."

"Hum or sigh?"

Hagar took a sip of Coke to clear her thoughts. "Both at the same time, I guess. I don't know, I can't explain it. But I don't like it."

Vilonsky didn't like it either, but what did Hagar know from Jerusalem rabbis? It was that atavism at work again. She was too young to have earned the right to such feelings. "I'll try not to sigh again, Hagar," Vilonsky vowed, and made a mental note of it. "Now eat up your cake."

Hagar held up an empty plate. "All gone," she said. A few minutes later, Vilonsky solicited a kiss from his granddaughter and sent her home.

It is hard to walk the streets of Tel Aviv and long for invisibility, but Vilonsky longed for it all the same. By nature a man of introspection, he enjoyed losing himself in thought several times a day, especially on Tuesday afternoons, en route to meet his granddaughter at Café Schweitzer. On such a day, the retrieval of long-forgotten memories often came to his aid. (The termination of his strolls with Sylvia along the Yarkon River coincided with the construction of the Reading Power Station along its banks. The insult of industrial effluents: that's why she'd stopped coming! It wasn't him at all.)

Vilonsky resented living in a city that forced him to observe things external to his own self: first the beggar and now—what was this?—a crowd of people gaping at an illegally parked car. Splendid.

Vilonsky approached the crowd. "What's the big spectacle?" he asked a woman brandishing a stick.

"Can't you see? This family's driveway is blocked by that crappy Nissan. Look at those poor kids in the Renault. They needed to be in Haifa an hour ago for their cousin's wedding."

Vilonsky looked. An old Renault sputtered in the driveway, a family of five sitting impatiently in it, revved up but redundant, like the car engine hindered from doing its work. Sitting behind the wheel was the mother, staring in disbelief at the inert vehicle a few feet away; next to her the father, screaming into a cell phone above the cries of the children from the backseat.

"*Nu?* Honk your horn!" someone suggested. "The driver might be across the street at the *makolet*."

The mother shrugged, then threw her weight against the horn.

A finger wagged a response. "What are you honking

for? You think the driver would risk being towed for a kilo of tomatoes? He was probably late for work, and didn't even notice the driveway."

Vilonsky's patience was wearing thin. He had only one more question for the woman brandishing the stick. "Excuse me, but what are you planning to do with that?"

"The stick?" Its holder was happy someone had noticed, having forgotten about it herself. "The drivers in this country have gone too far, and I'm going to show them once and for all. Go ahead, Lior. Show them."

A man stepped forward, a large dog of unidentifiable breed at his side, and scratched the dog under its chin, causing it to release a red object from its mouth.

"Voilà!" Lior shouted, and hurled a tooth-marked pomegranate at the windshield. Vilonsky closed his eyes.

"Bravo!" came a cry of approval.

"Who's gone too far, you golem? Get out of here with your stupid dog!"

"But he's right to teach that driver a lesson."

"What lesson? He obviously didn't see the driveway when he parked."

"Or the white stripes staring him in the face?"

"Didn't see the forest for the trees, you mean."

"What forest? You've got a screw loose, lady."

"*Nu,* Sarit. I did the dirty work. Now paint your picture already."

As the stick sprang into action, Vilonsky opened his eyes and cringed at the sight of the red Rorschach blot splashed against the windshield. This was a far cry from the Latvian artist he had read about in a weekend edition of *Haaretz*, whose sculpture of human feces was being hailed as a commentary on modern consumption. Such an impulse he could accept, with its critique of excess and plea to make the world a better place, unfettered by the borders of our own making. But his own countrymen . . . the woman's stick like a weapon in the hands of a child, her abstract smears expressing nothing but disdain . . . a curse devoid of commentary. Vilonsky glanced at the portrait as it neared completion. In a reversal of priorities, he wished for a downpour to come to the aid of the missing driver, a rare summer rain to wash the slate of his conscience clean.

A tow truck was crawling down the street now, oblivious to the urgency of the situation. Vilonsky shifted his attention to the truck and for a second was fixated, though by what he did not know. The driver was munching on an apple—was that it? The incongruity of the apple? His other arm hung limply out the window—was that it? The sight of a truck advancing on autopilot?

The crowd clapped as the tow truck hitched the Nissan to its back, but only Vilonsky stayed to see it hauled away.

To avoid additional distractions, Vilonsky turned into the nearest alley. The scent of citrus accompanied him as he walked, its source a grove of lemon trees planted in respectable rows. Vilonsky inhaled; was it under a lemon tree near his childhood home in Zichron that Sarah Aaronsohn had shot herself, or by a grapevine? During the last years of her life, after succumbing to dementia, his mother had spoken incessantly of the suicide, as if she had been part of the NILI spy ring herself, her carrier pigeon captured and code cracked by the Ottoman forces in the area. Vilonsky inhaled again; on the balcony of a house stood a Filipina live-in pouring out a bucket of sudsy water onto the grass below. The fumes confounded him; his thoughts couldn't coalesce. How old had his mother been in 1917? Perhaps the dementia had simply been another distraction, a handy tool to prevent the truth from coming to light? He couldn't rule out the possibility.

Mohnkuchen: the German (or was it Yiddish?) word for poppy-seed cake, bandied about by a number of Vilonsky's relatives during Rosh Hashanah every year, until his grandmother died and the baking ceased.

Miriam, es brennt was!

Was brennt?

Soll ich wissen? Der Mohnkuchen!

Ach, der Mohnkuchen!

Something was always burning in the Vilonsky oven; once the door was closed, Grandmother Vilonsky abdicated her post and went into the living room to take a nap. Having grown up in Zichron, where the presence of its founder, Baron Edmond James de Rothschild, was still felt in every home, Vilonsky was not averse to limited European influence on his native tongue; *Mohnkuchen* was a household word back then because it made sense, just as carp swimming in the Vilonsky bathtub in preparation for a Sabbath meal made sense. Hagar loved her cake best with a slice of mango on the side, a request that cafés only sometimes could accommodate. *Mohnkuchen* and mangoes—it had a nice ring to it, Vilonsky had to admit, especially as he passed a mango tree on his way out of the alley and tried out the phrase a few times under his breath. But to introduce a foreign phrase to Hagar simply for the way it sounded, without context? It didn't make sense. And to introduce it with context—for Vilonsky to pry his parents' oven open again after so many years—made even less sense. The girl had never been to Zichron.

Vilonsky sighed, then turned toward the nearest *makolet* to buy his granddaughter a mango.

The way was short, the sidewalk a steady stream of cyclists eschewing the bicycle lane. Vilonsky kept his head down, noting with disapproval the number of feet filling the wrong lane, while in his own lane the wheels whizzed by chaotically. Vilonsky braced himself for a collision and carefully prepared his responses to any curses that might come his way. *You can use that little bell of yours for room service when you visit me in the hospital!* he would shout at the next person who tried to ring him into the wrong lane. *What's that, young man? I should open my eyes? If I were you, I would keep yours closed when you get my hospital bill!*

Vilonsky grinned as the verbal sparring in his head evolved into an outright battle of wits, and declared himself victor several minutes in. When he bent down to tie his shoe, a bicycle missed him by a hairbreadth, and he called after the culprit, "Don't think I didn't see you, boychick!" This surprised Vilonsky as much as it would have surprised the cyclist, had the latter slowed down enough to hear it. Would the man have recognized the word as a term of endearment, or taken Vilonsky to task for the intended insult? Was using a Yiddish word in itself an insult in the first Hebrew city of Tel Aviv? Vilonsky remembered the years when it had been.

The *makolet* was matchbox small, the mangoes easy to spot, arranged in an imperfect pyramid at the back of the store. Vilonsky stood before the display and thought twice before disturbing it, so precariously were the items placed; a two-for-one deal made the risk of avalanche even greater.

With the tips of his fingers, Vilonsky plucked a fruit from the top of the pile, then a second one, as deftly as the first.

Voilà!

He carried them like two newborn babies to the scale to be weighed.

Only two other customers stood in line with Vilonsky, one in front and one behind; to his relief, neither said a word. When he placed his fruits-of-the-week on the scale, the cashier quickly removed them, holding his customer's babies up to the light as if to check for jaundice.

"Avocado?"

"Mango," Vilonsky corrected.

"Then why's it green?"

"Green, but ready to eat." Vilonsky demonstrated with a thumb-poke. "And at two for one, they're a steal."

The cashier frowned. "Green and ripe? That changes everything. The deal was for green and not ripe. I thought they were avocados."

"I see," said Vilonsky. "How much, please?"

"Five shekels if you go take the sign down. I've got a bum foot."

Ask Hagar about a Maya mango, and she would tell you from which kibbutz near the Sea of Galilee they came, how they were harvested, and the export price per kilo. But the customer behind him—what was she prattling on about?

"Maybe it's a mangocado."

"A mangocado?" the cashier repeated. He deposited Vilonsky's money into the cash register, then slammed the drawer shut without retrieving any change. "Mister, you ever heard of that?"

With Hagar's five shekels in his pocket, Vilonsky could have spared himself the present situation and arrived at Café Schweitzer with a clear head. But he had something to say.

"Darwin observed that soup dripping from a man's beard is disgusting, even though beard and soup are not themselves disgusting. A hybrid fruit such as the one you are proposing would appeal to no one."

The customer behind Vilonsky was now in front of him, a loaf of bread tucked under her arm. "A party pooper, that's what you are," she said, zipping her purse and heading out the door. "We were just having some fun."

"Just kidding around," added the cashier with a broad smile. His fingers landed on and gripped Vilonsky's shoulder. "You enjoy those mangocados now, and don't forget where they came from." As if of its own volition, the cash register popped open again, and Vilonsky untethered himself to accept its offering.

Outside once more, Vilonsky accelerated his steps. He was close enough to Café Schweitzer now to face any final obstacles with humor, to consider the distractions that awaited him in a different light. A cigarette butt, tossed from a scaffolding, landing at his feet? The ever-evolving interpretation of workers' rights! Three electric scooters shunting him off the sidewalk and onto Yehuda Hamaccabi Street just as three buses hurtled past? Never mind, good things came in threes: a genie's wishes, notes in a chord. And, of course, the number three corresponded to the letter *gimel* in gematria—a letter resembling, with its foot at the base, a man in motion, like Vilonsky himself on this helter-skelter day. Yes, things had a way of adding up when you put your mind to it. . . .

But the incident at the *makolet*—the idea of taking nature's most perfect fruit (Hagar's fruit) and turning it into some horrid hybrid, a new species in an already-sated world—just kidding around, were they? Then why not kid about something else, a situation that lent itself to levity, such as a driveway blocked by an absent-minded driver in search of a tomato? Anyone could find the humor in that, and yet no one had. The hysterical reaction, battling a phantom enemy with rotten fruit, a population of noise polluters fraying the nerves of the country with their big mouths—and Vilonsky in the middle, sucked into the epicenter of all that senseless honking and shouting . . .

The smell of hot coffee called him back to the sidewalk. A few more steps and he would be sitting at a table with his granddaughter, eating mangoes and *Mohnkuchen* and catching each other up on the events of the past week. Vilonsky couldn't wait to tell Hagar about the crazy things he had experienced this morning, experiences he had not sought out but had been sucked into against his will, like a fly trapped in a honey jar. The metaphor wasn't perfect (the city had lost its sweetness years before), but until a better one came to him . . .

A sharp pain shot through Vilonsky's ankle as he tripped on the curb and tumbled to the sidewalk.

"Oy!"

"What happened? A car?"

"The curb."

"Here, give me your hand."

"No, take his other hand."

"Oy!" Vilonsky cried out again. He heard a swirling of voices around him. "My coin!"

"Coin? Maybe he needs an ambulance. Mister, should we call you an ambulance?"

"He doesn't need an ambulance. He just needs to get up. Mister, can you try to stand up?"

But Vilonsky didn't want to stand up. Hagar's coin had fallen out of his pocket and rolled away, down the gutter or into the hands of a passerby—or into the spokes of a bicycle, the claws of a cat—it didn't matter where, it was gone, and in an hour Hagar would be gone too, having forgotten to bring (yet again) a coin for the parking meter . . . always the same excuse . . . but today Vilonsky had remembered. Today Hagar would have stayed, even after the time on the meter ran out, even if the tow truck driver had chewed his apple down to the core and spit out the seeds.

"*Saba?* What happened? I was waiting inside. Give me your hand."

Hagar stood over him, a grown woman of nearly thirty, and still not married.

"Hagar."

"Give me your hand, *Saba.*"

Hagar, his only granddaughter, born in an age of excess and yet an only child, her mother convinced that the world was not expanding but contracting, and that soon it would stop being hospitable to humankind and retreat into itself, like the self-exile of the Shechinah after the destruction of the Temple in Jerusalem. Alona had been attending classes at the new kabbalah center in Jaffa. Where else would these ideas have come from? Surely not from Vilonsky, who had always tried to protect his daughter from the negative influences around them, from the big mouths bent on changing others' minds after they had already been made up.

Unless, somewhere along the way, he had taken the wrong step (as now) and contributed to Alona's confusion? His divorce certainly hadn't helped, not to speak of the renewal of war every few years, the fear of a military with ever-more-frightening weapons. When, as a child, Alona had once asked if she could invite a friend over the next day, Vilonsky had tried not to project his fears about what the next day might bring and joked instead that she shouldn't wait so long, because by tomorrow her friend might have grown a tail or a sharp beak. Had that thoughtless quip been the cause of Alona's bad dreams during that vulnerable period of her childhood? And had those bad dreams led to a bad marriage years later, and to Hagar's being deprived of a sibling to sleep next to?

Slowly, painstakingly, Vilonsky unclenched his fingers and discovered a five-shekel coin implanted in his palm like a pacemaker.

"The mangoes," he groaned. The coin was safe but the mangoes were gone.

"What mangoes?"

The mangoes were gone, and with them the *Mohnkuchen* that might have been resurrected. Vilonsky had thought, on this final stretch toward Café Schweitzer, that the word might find favor with the girl after all—the word, and some of the stories associated with it. But his foot was throbbing, the pain muddling his plan.

"What mangoes, *Saba*?" Hagar asked again.

It was a question that cried out for an answer.

Two Passions for Two People

Igor can draw the flight posture of an egret in his sleep: wings partially folded to lower air resistance, toes locked in place, body long and sleek and straight as an arrow. I can draw it too.

He's been at it for months now: cranes, herons, finches, even the common yellowthroats he grew up with in Russia. He studies them all, loves them all, loves America for letting him love them. He claims that studying birds is essential to his survival. When I threaten to move out, he shrugs.

Over breakfast, Igor suggests that I too cultivate a hobby. "While I study, you can study," he says with enthusiasm. "Two passions for two people."

I sign up for a class in first aid. The instructor asks us what we'd like to learn about most: eye, neck, or back injuries, or wounds of the chest. I vote for all of them.

The others are less eager. One student admits that he has come only for swimming safety tips, another that he would rather be playing Frisbee. Soon there is a compromise. By the end of the day I have written in my notebook, "Injuries to the genital organs may result from kicks, blows, straddle accidents involving machinery, and occasionally strikes from sharp instruments. Such injuries are accompanied by great pain."

For two weeks I let my new passion lead me. My skin softens and my breasts swell. The gauze pads reserved for class absorb the moisture collecting at my brow. Igor takes notice, stops what he is doing, and follows me into the bedroom. For an hour we lie together without talking. Like the turkey vulture, we make only an occasional grunt or hiss.

I call my mother, and for a moment things return to normal. "I've been in your shoes a hundred times," she assures me. "All you need is a little attention."

"From who? Igor?"

"From you, from yourself," my mother says confidently. "Try it for a day, and you'll see."

I try it for more than a day. I throw away my tourniquet and my tweezers and the remainder of my gauze pads, and give myself over to me. Gradually my senses sharpen. When I am in the supermarket pushing a cart, I feel the movement of every muscle, and I say, "That's me." When I stand before a sculpture in a museum and pause to run my fingers along the cold bronze surface, a warmth rises up, and I say, "That's me."

Igor takes notice of the change by coming home late. But when my mother calls, I tell her I am not through with myself, that there is still more attention to be given.

"One day is the limit," she insists. "More than that and you're lost. Trust me, I know."

I balk at her words. "I'm not going to stop."

"Oh, yes you are. You'll start flubbing things up if you don't. Yesterday I saw Mrs. Brody, and she said Abby has given up taxis for buses. Nobody knows why. Go outside and trim the hedges, and you'll be all right."

I take to the streets. First I pass people, then only storefronts. I stop at a store and buy a pair of wire clippers, then continue on until I see a taxi parked behind a bus. I look at one, then at the other. Whatever the difference is, I can't see it. I walk back and forth between the two vehicles, trying to make up my mind. When the bus begins to pull away from the curb, I board it.

At the city's outskirts, I see a sign for the zoo and get off at the next stop. Nearing the entrance, I see a second sign. It reads, "The zoo's grounds and all its inhabitants belong to the American people. 1891."

The first structure I come to is the reptile house. I gaze up at its red tile roof and pull open a pair of massive oak doors. Inside are sculpted panels of crocodiles, turtles, frogs, and snakes. I ask an attendant where the elephants are, and he leads me back out again.

Within fifteen minutes, I have fed peanuts to an elephant and peered into the mouth of a rhinoceros. Within half an hour, I have seen a river otter squeeze himself dry along the narrow rubber entrance to his den, and a baby short-tailed bat cling to the shirt of a zookeeper like a brooch.

I am avoiding the birds.

I make my way to the concession stand. The man in front of me orders twelve bags of peanuts and a Coke. Clutching a cup of ice water, I sit down next to an old woman at a table. She too has ordered peanuts and is busily removing each one from its shell. I watch as two distinct piles accumulate in front of us, then inform her that some animals actually prefer the shell to the nut, and that without the shell, according to a brochure at the information desk, there is an increased risk of intestinal parasites.

The woman ignores me and mutters something under her breath. When she has finished shelling the last peanut, she scoops up all the nuts and shoves them into her mouth.

I leave the concession stand drained of energy. Not trusting myself, I follow a family of six in and out of simulated landscapes and public restrooms. When one of the children squeals at a polar bear catching a fish, I squeal. When the mother stops to shake a pebble from her shoe, I discover a pebble in my shoe. Before long we have arrived at a towering constellation of six arches connected by wire netting. As we approach it, I feel my stomach drop, and the smallest of the boys runs forward, shouting, "The bird house! The bird house!"

I separate myself from the family and begin to walk slowly, like a predator, around the flight cage. At the far end a flock of yellow birds has congregated in front of an open hand disseminating pieces of bread through the wire. When the birds disperse, I see Igor, clapping his hands free of excess crumbs. "Igor," I say when I reach him. "What are you doing at the zoo?"

Igor's eyes dart back and forth, following the path of the birds. "I'm studying bill shapes," he says, finally turning toward me. "This is where I always come."

I rest the clippers on a link in the fence. "You come to the zoo to watch birds in captivity? Why don't you buy a pair of binoculars? Why don't you buy a field guide?"

Igor does not understand my exasperation. He shrugs. "I've always come here." He returns to his usual enthusiasm. "Today I saw a barn swallow scoop an insect right out of the air. His bill is too thin to crush seeds, and too short to probe the ground. But it's perfect for catching flying things, flat with a broad base. He wouldn't take a single crumb from my hand."

Together we circle the parabolic structure, Igor pointing out the birds and explaining their various habits. After we have made two complete rounds, I stop at the entrance to the cage, clippers in hand, and turn to him. "I have come to free the birds, Igor," I say. "To release them from their captivity."

Igor stares at the clippers, stunned. He takes a few steps backward and sits down on a bench.

I watch him scratch little bird's feet into the ground with a stick. "Don't worry, you'll find a new hobby," I say comfortingly. "America is a big country."

As I cut out a hole in the wire netting, dozens of birds shy away to the corners of the cage, as if convening a meeting. But a few hop toward the widening gap, and I call out to them, prompting Igor to stand up and drop his stick.

"Step away from the cage, Igor," I gently instruct. Igor complies, and I walk with him toward the reptile house, guiding him with my free hand. Behind us, I hear the birds sing and flap their wings, and I turn around once to gauge the direction of their flight. I do not tell Igor which way they have gone.

A Famine in the Land

I knew I was in for a treat when Peter sent me to the IGA for a bunch of parsley. Nobody goes to the IGA for parsley; I would be the first. Peter was enjoying a first of his own at home, standing in front of a pot with a chicken in it and waiting for something magical to happen. And parsley is the most magical of herbs. A single sprig in your mouth, and all the difficult things you had been daring yourself to say to your spouse no longer need be said: you have been cleansed.

I was not in any particular hurry, but the paved hill that led to the IGA was the running-down kind so I ran, ending up out of breath at the bottom and smack in front of the store window, to which so many fliers were taped it was hard to tear my eyes away: "Are you using crack or cocaine?" "Have you recently stopped drinking alcohol?" "Would you like to quit smoking?" "Yellow Cab is hiring new drivers! Unlimited pay potential!" "Praise the Lord Jesus at the Tonsler Park hay maze!" As if in preparation for entering the store, I read them all.

It was dim inside the IGA, the kind of dimness I had never come across in other stores, the kind that seemed more conducive to shoplifting than to shopping. The lights were on, but were of such low wattage as to encourage a small release of melatonin into my brain with every step I took. Sleepily I made out a sign above a deep freezer that said "FRESH FISH" and walked toward it, inhaling the air around me and hoping it would jolt me back to wakefulness.

The sign said "FRESH FISH," but I distinctly saw diapers. And socks. And baby bibs. I didn't need fish any more than I needed diapers, socks, or baby bibs, because Peter had never put *baby* on a shopping list. Mr. Lee must have seen the disappointment on my face because he came to my aid at once.

"What you looking for?" he asked.

"Parsley," I said.

"Come with me," he said, and I didn't hesitate because I knew what a treat I was in for (Koreans being such good cooks), a treat surpassing the cavernous wanderings of a customer sent to the IGA in search of something green. I could already smell the oil heating up for the omelet and wondered whether Mrs. Lee would know how much I loved kimchi just by looking at me, though only the kind you get from Trader Joe's. Anything hotter than that would require an explanation. Mr. Lee stopped in front of a rack of plastic packets from Mexico so randomly ordered, I almost had trouble distinguishing cinnamon sticks from double-A batteries. Everything seemed to blend together after a single glance, and why were we not advancing toward the kitchen?

Mr. Lee unhooked a bag containing the shriveled brain of a very small animal.

"What's that?" I asked, though it hardly mattered to me what kind of animal it was. What mattered was that Mrs. Lee was not in the kitchen at all, but sitting in a Western Union kiosk, watching television.

"Ginger," said Mr. Lee.

I have two friends named Bonnie, which is two friends named Bonnie more than anyone should have. The last time I saw the first Bonnie, she had become a vegetarian after her son brought home a veiltail betta fish and named him Oscar.

"Are those the kind of fish that can breathe air and live in rice paddies?" I'd asked her, vaguely recalling such a fish via those two small facts associated with it.

But Bonnie remembered even less than that, and still she was committed. "You know," she said impatiently, forming indistinct shapes with her hands. "Like those fish you see at Walmart? That kind."

I wondered what kind of changes my encounter with Mr. Lee would compel me to adopt. Mr. Lee observed me wondering this and returned the brain to its place, next to a bag of clothespins.

"OK," he said, and I understood what he meant: *Enough. Go home to your husband, where you belong. He is in the attic, playing the accordion.*

And that's just where Peter was, because everyone has longings.

"OK," I said, and tried to size up the rest of the store before my departure. I saw cans of beans, rolls of toilet paper, boxes of cereal, and numerous bare shelves that in another place would have signified happy households well stocked with beans, toilet paper, and cereal, but here evoked a barren landscape with no back orders on the way.

"I guess I'll buy a lottery ticket," I said, which I did, a scratch card pitting sunflowers against zombies. It got me closer to Mrs. Lee and the image on her black-and-white television screen: a beautiful Korean woman in a white robe on her knees and drinking from a bowl of dark liquid while a small group of royal guards, also in white robes, encircled her in a courtyard. I stood at the Western Union window and watched as the empty bowl fell to the ground and the poison took effect to the accompaniment of zithers, transforming the young woman's face into a twisted knot of pain. I thought of a story Peter had once told me about a hazing incident in Ohio that left an eighteen-year-old student dead, an empty bottle of soy sauce cradled in his lap like a lucky charm.

"The boy had his whole life ahead of him," he'd said. We must have both wanted a baby so badly then.

*

It was a challenge keeping my bar mitzvah student awake. Sam liked our leather couch, where we sat once a week, a bright yellow folder with multiple Hebrew pages sticking out straddling our laps. I didn't mind that he usually smelled of school and unbrushed braces, or that he had trouble pronouncing the chet; but when his mind went blank midsentence and his eyes closed, I cursed his parents for not enforcing a proper bedtime, and then myself for not knowing when that might be. Nine o'clock? Ten? How many hours did a preteen require these days? It was not enough to know that I needed twelve.

"Should we talk about the parashah before we start?" I suggested.

"Sure," Sam said, but neglected to sit up even an inch straighter.

"Remember when Joseph gets thrown into the pit by his brothers, and ends up in Egypt as a slave?"

"Not really. I never went to Sunday school. My sister did, but I had soccer."

"You wouldn't have learned that at Sunday school," I said. "At Sunday school you would have learned how to feed a cat at the SPCA. But whatever. Forget the 'remember' part. The point is that Joseph interprets Pharaoh's dream and predicts there's going to seven years of plenty in Egypt, followed by seven years of famine. But how could he know this?"

I had been testing out a crazy theory about Joseph for days already, seeking out Peter as my springboard and insisting on eye contact even after deflecting criticism about the cheddar cheese I had bought.

"I like that you're asking me about crop rotation," Peter had said, utterly serious, which was good, because I wasn't trying to be funny. I was trying to understand why Joseph, in charge of the land, did not let it rest after reaping—as was the custom—but instead "gathered in its yield, like the sands of the sea," over and over, until the land ceased to be productive. "But you're too impatient to listen."

And I was, so much so that I took my husband's least favorite cheese from the table and threw it into the sink, doing us both a favor.

"Just tell me if you think Joseph, who had been a farmer in Canaan and knew a lot about agriculture, hoarded the country's crops in order to cause the famine?"

Peter was intrigued. "Go on," he said.

But I clammed up, because we were working well together at that moment, and the next moment was only a sentence away.

"Never mind."

"No, tell me."

"It's too complicated."

*

Sam was considerably more awake now; you could actually see the color of his eyes. "You mean, like stealing? Nobody really steals food," he said. "Unless it's a pack of gum or something."

Or unless you know the famine will spread to Canaan and cause your father, whom you have not seen in twenty years, to come looking for you, the bonds of love between parent and child having grown more intense over time. That's what I had wanted to say to Peter, who had stopped asking for herbs when he cooked, settling for salt and pepper as poor substitutes.

*

Going to Mark and Lia's always reminded me how I loved the children Peter and I didn't have infinitely more than the children friends expected us to indulge when we went to their houses for dinner. Peter and I sank into the couch while Walker and Eve danced around us, delighted by the gift we had brought for them until they unwrapped it and saw what it was: a book by that creepy Roald Dahl. *Charlie and the Chocolate Factory* had unsettled their sleep, Walker said, and here it was again!

"We *have* this already," Eve said sternly, and handed it back.

Peter was waiting for Mark to open the good wine we had entrusted him with, but I was fairly confident it had already been buried in the backyard, to be dug up and enjoyed on a different occasion. "Why, thank you, Eve. Now I do too," Peter said distractedly, taking the book back with just enough conviction to compete with Roald Dahl's creepiness and drive the kids out of the room. "I smell something in the oven."

I sniffed the air. "They might be serving more than soup this time."

"Did you notice Mark's hair?"

"It's totally dyed," I said, a fact I might have failed to notice if I had a baby at home, waiting to be breast-fed.

"Didn't he used to live on a commune and make hammocks?"

"He certainly did."

"So how can he dye his hair?"

"He didn't just make hammocks. Tofu too."

"Does that make it better?"

"No, worse," I assured my husband.

An hour later, we sat around the table eating thin lentil soup. The smell from the oven was growing stronger, even as I was beginning to suspect there was nothing in it.

"I checked the seventh-grade reading list at Eve's school, and *The Diary of Anne Frank* isn't on it," Lia lamented, salting her soup liberally, then passing the shaker to me like a side dish.

"Isn't Eve in fourth grade?"

Lia smiled; she just couldn't help herself. "She's a very advanced reader," she said. "But if no one is reading *The Diary of Anne Frank* anymore, then maybe she shouldn't either. It changes you so profoundly, and then you're immersed in that world of horror for weeks afterward. If she's the only one of her friends experiencing that—"

"We could let her read it but stress the 'I believe every person is good at heart' part," suggested Mark.

"If you do that, you might as well tell her Anne Frank survived, and is living in Brooklyn," I said, staring right at Mark's scalp.

"Didn't someone write a novel to that effect?" Peter said, breaking his silence.

"Mom, is the pizza ready yet?"

It is remarkable how quiet kids can be when they know something good has been conditionally promised them. I had hardly even noticed Eve and Walker sitting with us, even after Walker turned over his unfilled soup bowl and placed it on his head. They were not fans of lentil soup, Lia explained as she slid the pizza onto a cutting board and sliced it into four small pieces. Of any soup, actually. Wasn't that odd?

And just as quickly as it had been taken out of the oven, our dinner disappeared onto two plates and into the playroom, like evidence whisked away from a crime scene.

How Peter could have even thought about making love that evening when we returned home, hungry and humiliated, I don't know; I didn't go for that idea one bit.

"I want an Annie's pizza," I said, climbing out of bed still fully clothed, the way I sleep when the day has been unkind to me.

"Does it have to be Annie's?"

"Yes, or something frozen, with that processed smell."

"Can it be dumplings?" Peter asked, as if we were playing a game of twenty questions. "I think we have some in the freezer."

"It has to be pizza," I insisted. "Crappy frozen pizza."

"Try the IGA," Peter suggested.

So I did.

It was dark, of course, and Peter should have come with me. We had been holding hands lately, after I'd read about the benefits of hand-holding during open heart surgery. It approximated the real thing. At the top of the paved hill I considered turning around and going back, trading one impulsive move for another, but then I caught a whiff of something hot and greasy coming from a kitchen close enough to put things in perspective again, and I charged down the hill like the hungry, angry bull that I was, imagining the soles of my feet spraying sparks of justice into the air.

But I was not alone at the bottom, and justice isn't always so easy to find. A man in a hoodie stood outside the entrance, in the same spot where I had lingered the time before, trying to make sense out of pleas posted for other people, words that were now too dim to impart any wisdom. I nodded to him and he nodded back, stepping in front of me after doing so, as if to secure his place in a line we were not yet in.

"Get the fuck out of here," he said, flicking his neck to show me which way was out: back up the hill and home to Peter.

It is only natural to freeze for a moment before running for your life, which is what I did, froze, but only for a moment, just long enough to set my eyes on the first handgun I'd seen that was not attached to a policeman's hip. I did not like the way it looked, like a spare part salvaged from a scrap yard, or the way the man looked when he lifted his hood over his head to become someone else, someone he was not meant to be.

"I said, get the fuck out of here. Go home to your kids."

Sometimes, when you run as fast as your legs can carry you, you feel as if you are running in slow motion, as if in a dream where you are being pursued, or where you are in pursuit of something just out of reach, like a love letter with the last line crossed out. Mr. Lee was not a rich man; anyone who had ever been in his store knew that. Perhaps the man with the gun needed food for his family, I reasoned at the top of the hill, where I tried to catch my breath. My bar mitzvah student was wrong: people did steal food, and maybe that explained why so many of the shelves at the IGA were bare, because people were hungry, and not everyone wanted to clean out a small businessman's cash register. Because they understood that Mr. Lee was hungry too.

And then I heard a gunshot, and I stopped reasoning.

That bastard, with his snide comment; didn't he understand that some of us have only ourselves to feed, and that some things can't be put on a shopping list? By the time the police came, I was too worked up to be a witness, carrying on incoherently about babies and bad pizza, Anne Frank and wine bottles buried in the ground. With a trembling hand, I tried to point out the tacked-up signs by the store entrance; if the officers would only read them, they would stop asking so many stupid questions. Poor Mr. Lee: he had thought he was doing a good deed by putting them up.

The Gown

The nurse came in to check my blood pressure wearing a hospital gown. I stared at her out of one eye, then the other, trying to assess what was wrong. When she saw me look up, she raised a hand to fix her hair; when my eyes fell to her shoes, she bent down to remove a tissue from the floor.

I held out my arm for her to cuff. "Is that a hospital gown you're wearing?" I finally asked.

The nurse pressed a button and the band took hold. "A patient urinated on my dress," she explained.

I looked at the nurse's gown and tried to imagine the dress she might have been wearing a short time before, its stiff white collar concealing the curve of her neck, the buttons fixed in front and evenly spaced, like a row of turnips planted in a garden. I sensed that she was lying, that there were many alternatives to wearing a hospital gown, and she had chosen to ignore them all. When my arm was free again, I used it to bring my own gown closer to my body. "Why do you need to check my blood pressure so often?" I asked. "I feel like I'm in shackles all day."

The nurse collected her kit and stood up to leave. "You are," she said, eyeing herself in the mirror on her way out. "You just had a baby."

After I had fed my baby a few times, my gown stayed open. Nurses shuffled in and out, some to check my blood pressure, others to adjust my IV. All of them wore pants. The hand that I had used to cover up now lay limp by my side, too weak to work. At one in the morning, just as I was finally drifting off, a man in overalls came in to change a lightbulb.

In my half sleep I watched him climb a ladder and remove the burned-out bulb from above the television. I did not ask who had sent him. Instead I said, "Oh, that's great, thanks a lot," and tried to adjust my eyes to the bright light that was assaulting them.

The man swung around on the ladder to face me, then quickly swung back again at the sight of my open gown. "Want me to turn it off?" he asked, snapping the plastic cover into place.

The man's discomfort puzzled me. A baby had been pulled from my belly, and from that moment on my body existed for that baby alone. I rolled a nipple casually between my fingers until a drop of milk emerged and said, "No, you can keep it on."

When my baby was brought in from the nursery for his next feeding, I hadn't slept in over twenty-four hours. My head was spinning and when I tried to lift it, I heard myself say to the nurse, "Did you know that Cleopatra owned an emerald mine on the Red Sea?"

The nurse leaned over my bed and showed me how to keep the baby from kicking my incision. "Hold him like a football," she said, cradling his head in her palm. "And when he's finished eating, cover up so you don't catch a chill."

At these instructions, I felt my head spin even faster. "I'm too tired to cover up," I said. "Which way is up?"

Sometime after lunch I summoned the strength to limp to the window. I had not seen the sky since my baby was born, and I wanted to see the sky. The pain from my incision would not permit me to stand up straight, and by the time I reached the window my gown had slipped off my shoulders and onto the floor.

I leaned against the glass and looked out. Big clouds hung in the air. I thought of my baby, sleeping in the nursery, and tried to imagine what he would see looking at the same image. In a few years I would tell him to find animals in the clouds, and he would: bear, cat, rabbit, snake. And a few years after that, when I still saw only bear, cat, rabbit, snake, he would see more: an Alaskan brown bear catching a salmon with its paw; an elephant stirring up insects for an egret; a flamingo making a mud nest.

As I stared at the sky, the door opened and a doctor walked in. "I've come to remove your staples," he said. "But I can come back later."

"Don't be silly," I replied, heading back to my bed. The doctor fixed his eyes on a fruit basket while I climbed in, then walked over to the window to pick up my gown from the floor. "Do you want to put this back on?" he asked.

I touched a hand to my belly. "Maybe after the staples are out. My incision is beginning to itch."

One by one the doctor removed the staples, dropping them with a clink into a Dixie cup on his lap. I lay perfectly still and tried to shut my eyes, but the closer I came to sleep, the louder the clinks became. I asked the doctor whether it was necessary to drop the staples into a cup and told him a story I remembered from my grandmother about a small group of Russian tribesmen who used kopecks to fire on their enemies after running out of ammunition. "The surgeons who removed the coins from the corpses let them fall to the ground before collecting them," I explained. "Something about the sound of their impact helped clear the men's consciences."

The doctor held up the cup for me to peer into. "Sorry, just ordinary staples," he said. "But that's quite a story."

Later that afternoon my baby and I were discharged from the hospital. Nobody was waiting for us at home, only two dark rooms and a crib slept in by other babies before mine. I crawled into bed and stayed there for the rest of the day, getting up only to change a diaper or to try to move my bowels. I was not very successful at either.

Early in the evening, when darkness began to obscure the tiny body at my breast, the doorbell rang and my neighbor from across the hall stopped by, not to congratulate me or offer to hold the baby, but to borrow an egg.

"Jamal's birthday party is tonight," she said, brushing a hand over my baby's bald head, "and I got no time for nothing."

My neighbor went into the kitchen and returned with an egg and a stick of butter. "I didn't nurse Jamal, since I'm a smoker," she said, turning on a light and staring at my engorged breasts. "You finding it hard or easy?"

I glanced at the butter and the egg and tried to imagine the cake they would soon turn into. "I don't think anything will ever be easy again," I replied. "Do you know how to dress a wound or treat a burn?"

My neighbor pursed her lips and shook her head. "I hear you, baby. You think it's safe to leave a bag of hot dog buns on the table, and the minute you turn your head he's up to no good. It's the curse of curiosity."

I lifted my baby to my shoulder and tried to burp him. "Has Jamal ever swallowed a household cleaner?"

"Honey, you don't have to worry about that for some time yet. Your baby's legs are barely even kicking."

I looked at the egg in my neighbor's hand and tried to accept the truth in her statement. But I knew that to slow down the absorption of a poison, egg whites were often administered—and that she had just taken my last egg. For a moment I considered asking for it back; then a rush of air emerged from my baby's lungs and I asked her to order me a pizza instead.

I hadn't eaten since being released from the hospital. When the pizza arrived the baby was sleeping in his crib and the deliveryman, wearing a raincoat and tennis shoes, sat down in the living room while I fished around for some dollar bills. The clothes that I had worn in my last days of pregnancy were strewn about the apartment, and none of them seemed to have any pockets. Finally I gave up my search and asked if I could write a check.

"It's a dollar extra," the deliveryman said.

I wrote out a check for eleven dollars and placed it on the table. "How many pizzas do you get to take home every night?" I asked.

The deliveryman got up from the couch and unzipped a gray plastic pouch. "I could take home two of whatever's left, usually green pepper or onion, but I only eat food that existed in the time of the Bible, and pizza's not one of them."

I lifted a slice of pizza from the box. "That must be an incredible burden."

The deliveryman shrugged and walked around the room as I ate. "Nothing in life should be a burden," he said, pressing his nose against a bay window. "Least of all roast goose and dandelion greens, which the Good Book mentions by name."

As the deliveryman spoke, I heard a faint cry coming from the bedroom and felt a tingling in my armpits. "Excuse me for a minute," I said.

The baby kept his eyes closed while he nursed. I closed my eyes too and tried to concentrate on the milk draining from my breast. After every burst of sucks came a pause, and after every pause I felt the salt from the pizza rise to my tongue and rob it of moisture.

I opened my eyes and looked down at my baby, first at his hands, balled up like buds ready to bloom, and then at his flat feet cradled in the crook at my arm. His toes were idle, curled and stiff as though in the process of thawing out; the toenail on his pinky toe was the size of a grain of couscous. As a teenager I once saw a newborn calf rise to its wobbly feet and, after a few unsteady attempts, walk away from its mother to rub its head against a rock. I did not wonder, then, how the mother must have felt, watching her baby leave her soft side for a hard mass of stone. Instead I'd wondered how

I would feel sitting on that stone with the boy I had a crush on, the son of a Presbyterian minister, our legs sharing the same surface but not quite touching.

The deliveryman cast a shadow in the room. When I detected him behind me, I did not scream and press the baby against my body in a protective reflex. Nor did I ask him for a glass of water. Instead I stared at his raincoat and thought suddenly of my hospital gown, light and cool against my skin, its shapeless form a salve to my postpartum body. I was sorry I had left the gown at the hospital. I cringed at the thought that the healing process would take place all on its own, without supervision, and under clothing that bore the mark of the everyday world. "Come on in," I said to the deliveryman, jiggling my breast to keep the milk flowing. "I'm almost finished."

We played Monopoly, then cards. I lost at both. When he saw that I was getting tired, the deliveryman got up from the dining room table and stood directly in my line of vision. "If you want, we could bake cookies," he said eagerly. "Or a cake. I've got the rest of the night off. Do you have any figs?"

"My neighbor is throwing a birthday party for her son," I said, wishing I were there. "She took my last egg. There will be no cake tonight."

But the deliveryman stayed. He stayed and stayed and stayed. "Have you ever had a muskmelon?" he asked. "Do you want to watch TV?"

I remembered the advice of the nurse before I left the hospital—*if the baby doesn't wake himself for a feeding after four hours, do it for him*—and wondered who would wake me if I ever fell asleep.

At one o'clock in the morning, I finally asked the deliveryman to take off his raincoat. "Just pull it over your head," I said, irritated that it had so many buttons. "Just get rid of it."

With one swift motion the deliveryman pulled the snaps apart, hesitating on the last one as though fearful he might set something off underneath it. When the raincoat finally opened, he wriggled out of the sleeves and smoothed the outfit he was wearing underneath, an oversize sweatshirt that read, in big blue letters, "I'm not an alcoholic, I'm a drunk."

"I feel like I just performed a rain dance," the deliveryman said. He stomped his feet a few times, and I felt the floor tremble underneath me.

I nodded, then raised a finger to my lips and said, "Shhhh."

In silence I guided the deliveryman to the door. Pressing my hand against the small of his back, I pushed him forward, one step at a time, until the smell of cigarettes from across the hallway reached us where we stood.

I opened the door and sent the deliveryman away. "Good-bye," I said, in retreat. "I simply cannot keep my baby waiting any longer."

In the bedroom I spread the raincoat over my tired body. My baby did not wake up until the morning.

The Four Foods

My father is an imposing man. Small, with dark, sad eyes and gums that bleed when he brushes them in the morning. I ask my mother why he scares me so much. "It's his knowledge," she says. "He knows things."

I go out and buy a dictionary. I go out and buy textual sources for the study of world religions. History. Philosophy. The natural sciences. I craft concepts into sentences, theories into questions best asked over the telephone. I call my father. I say, "Dad?"

My mother tells me not to call him so often. "You're distracting him from his writing," she says. "Call me instead."

I cry into the phone. "You're so easy, and he's so hard."

"Now, honey." My mother tries to comfort me. "Now, pussycat."

We meet for lunch, my father and I. We sit across from each other like retirees and squint at the specials written in pink chalk above the counter.

Midway through our sandwiches we begin to talk. "Mom says she's allergic to goose feathers," I say. "What are you going to do with all the pillows from Europe?"

My father takes a sip of water. "Those pillows belonged to your great-grandmother. The feathers in them came all the way from Lvov."

I nod. "It's the shtetl. Mom doesn't want to go back."

My father sucks up a sesame seed through a gap

between his teeth, and I wait for him to acknowledge my analysis. For years, the pillows have reminded my mother that she has not always been an American. Now she is starting to sneeze whenever she gets near them.

"There is no shtetl anymore. There is no going back," my father says.

"But figuratively, the Old World—"

That evening, my mother scolds me over the phone. "There is no *figuratively*," she says. "Why do you always have to blab about what you don't know?"

"I thought we could talk about Europe or something—what it means to us."

"To us?"

"As Jews."

My mother thinks for a moment, then says, "Some Jews have allergies to feathers. I happen to be one of them. Burden your father with something else."

I sit in my apartment and stare at the wall. Through it I hear a brief hammering, then a silence, and then someone knocking at my door. I cannot pretend that it is anyone but Jake.

"Can you help me out a minute?" he says, pointing in the direction of his door, two pairs of bunny ears hanging from the toes of his house slippers.

While he nails a poster of Christie Brinkley to the wall, I lend Jake my eye. "Left," I say. "Left—OK, now right."

"Like this?"

"If it has to be."

I try to take the encounter at face value. I try to subtract the hammer and the house slippers and the bikini behind the glass, and see Jake for the ordinary man he is. "The picture looks good," I say.

Jake opens the refrigerator and pulls out a carton of milk. He drinks. "What do you have on your walls?"

I stare at the ring of milk above his mouth. "I'm waiting for just the right thing. A family picture, perhaps. Or maybe a picture of just my father, sitting at his typewriter. I would blow it up really big, and hang it in my living room."

Jake puts down the milk carton. "Are you serious?"

I imagine my father sitting at his typewriter, whacking at the keys with agitated fingers. I have never actually seen him do this; the door to his study is always closed. "Maybe I would put it in the bathroom," I say, reconsidering. "My father can only work in complete solitude."

*

My parents have me over for dinner. We sit around the kitchen table like a family and pass things: the salad, the bread, the soup bowls to be filled and then refilled. My father pours himself a glass of wine for his heart and asks, "Leah, have you been jogging lately?"

"I made a few rounds this morning," I say. "And I was thinking, if Leonard Bernstein was Jewish, why did he write a Mass?"

My father stares at his reflection in the soup. "I really don't know, honey."

I wait for more, but nothing comes. "Of course you know," I say. "You just don't feel like thinking when I'm around."

My mother deflects a frown by raising a napkin to her lips. "Leonard Bernstein is dead," she says firmly. "There's nothing to think about." She lowers the napkin and frowns anyway.

I turn to my father. He looks tired. A nerve twitches at his neck whenever he swallows, as though keeping time to some silent music. My father sees me looking and says, "You think a lot about Jews, don't you?"

I shrug. "I guess it runs in the family." My father has written many books, all of them about Jews.

"How about thinking about the family instead?" my mother suggests.

I want to explain to my father that I am trying to do just that, but he is already immersed in other, more intimate concerns, his eyes looking right at me but without registering a thing. Mahler's conversion to Catholicism? The expulsion from Spain? 1933? I am losing him. Again. Still.

*

I call my mother. I say, "It's not his knowledge. It's something else."

"It's *your* knowledge," my mother agrees. "It gets in the way."

"My knowledge? What do I know?"

"Nothing," my mother agrees. "That's the problem."

I go out and attend lectures, study forms and functions, foundations and first principles. I take notes while watching television. It is not a joke, I don't laugh. Usually I cry.

My mother calls me in the midst of it all. "Your father is in the hospital," she says. "He's got a hernia."

"Was it me?" I ask.

"It wasn't me," my mother says.

I visit my father in the hospital. He is lying in a small white bed in a small white room divided by a curtain. The nurse has parted his hair on the wrong side. My mother tells me to leave the curtain drawn; a very sick man is lying on the other side, and the separation will do my father good.

I look at my father, open my mouth, then close it again. My mother takes over. "How are you feeling, Howard?"

My father sticks out his tongue. "Ugh," he says.

I have never heard my father say *ugh* before. I repeat it. "Ugh?"

My mother pretends to smooth out a wrinkle in my father's sheet, and pinches me. "Ow!" I squeal.

My father opens his eyes a little wider. "Ow?"

Soon the nurse comes in to serve lunch. She places a plastic tray wrapped in aluminum foil on my father's lap, then disappears behind the curtain. I sit at the edge of my father's bed and remove the foil. Together we study the four compartments: chicken, broccoli, pears, water.

There is so much I want to say to my father at this moment, but I'm not sure where to begin, especially with my mother standing over me, at the ready. At the very least I want to tell him how good he looks in his hospital gown, like one of the high priests of the Temple in Jerusalem, before it was destroyed.

"You look good, Dad," I say, blinking away everything in the room but the robe. I am close enough to feel that it is cotton. "Like one of the *kohanim* in the *Beit Hamikdash.*"

I give my father a few seconds to answer, and when he doesn't, pick up the fork on his tray and slide it under a piece of chicken.

"What are you doing, Leah?" My mother tries to stop me, but I push her away. During visiting hours he is as much mine as anyone else's. Carefully I reach over and place the chicken into my father's mouth.

My father takes the food between his lips. He chews and chews and chews.

"How is the food, Howard?" my mother asks, still thinking I am flubbing it all up. "Is it too salty?"

Before he can answer, I break off two more pieces of chicken with my fingers. One piece I gently push into my father's mouth; the second piece I put into my own.

Together my father and I chew. We chew and chew and chew.

When we can chew no more, I look at my father and wait for a signal.

"*Nu*, how's the food, you pigs?" my mother asks again.

We swallow; my father belches. The stripes of his gown ripple under his raised belly.

Together we say, "Mmm."

Liliana, Years Later

If not for her name written neatly in pencil on the inside cover of my piano book, I might have forgotten that Liliana Szlenk ever existed, let alone changed my life. The line crossed through the z caught my eye first, followed by the L, which featured two loops that appeared almost embroidered onto the page, they were that lovely. Liliana was from Poland, and the book was the Chopin nocturnes, delicate and melancholy, just as Liliana herself had been. No études to evoke Warsaw rising in revolt against the tsar, or gloomy visions to remind Liliana that at thirty-five, she was nearly past childbearing age, and had no suitors to speak of.

When I first met Liliana, I was too young to master the music I was taught to play, and I am the first to admit that I played it poorly. But I was old enough to recognize, after every lesson, that I was not the same person I had been before the lesson, especially when Liliana moved to the middle of the piano bench and performed the piece from the top as if she had written it herself. She spoke a different language then, personal and private and hardly intended for me at all, like a monologue rehearsed in front of a mirror. But to my surprise, I understood every word of it.

I am now the age Liliana was when she first came to my house, a soft smile on her face that suggested no backstory, the smile of a recent immigrant to America from Poland who was not a Jew, the only non-Jewish immigrant from Poland I had ever met, and who I therefore assumed could not have a backstory at all.

"Of course she's not a survivor," my mother scoffed, at my question. "Liliana is going on forty, not eighty. But even at forty, not a line on her face. She's an immigrant, not a refugee."

"But she looks sad," I said.

"She's from Poland," my mother said.

"So she feels guilty for the Holocaust?"

"She hardly knows what a Jew is."

"So why is she sad?"

"Poland is a sad place without Jews," said my mother.

But of course my mother was clueless. Liliana never spoke of her broken heart, just as I do not speak of mine now, because when one tries to put pain into words, the words themselves become agents of new pain, like fresh paper cuts, and cannot be used again.

I was fifteen when she came for my first lesson, and instantly jealous of the large bosom she hid behind a blouse so modest, it was clear that wherever Poland was on the map, it was not near Paris. We shook hands (how finely trimmed her fingernails were!) and sat down at the piano bench as if we had sat on it together many times before.

"I hear you play Bach very well," Liliana said, and pointed to the book of Bach's Inventions that stayed permanently open to page five on the stand, because I liked to look at it every time I passed through the living room. All those black lines and dots were beautiful even without being decoded, and trying to play them more than was absolutely necessary would have been a pity.

But it was necessary to play them that day, and I placed my fingers on the keys so timidly that within a few minutes I could smell Liliana sweating under her modest blouse, a sweat that for some reason I associated with Poland despite not knowing where it was on the map.

"It's very nice," she lied when I was done.

"I should try not to say 'Wait' whenever I make a mistake," I considered.

"Yes," she agreed.

"Or maybe try not to make so many mistakes."

Closing the book, she reached into a plastic bag and removed another one with a hideous army-green cover.

"This is Chopin," she said.

The word sounded French, and she was no longer sweating. Liliana started to play, and the shadow in the room that had been my mother eavesdropping from around the corner gave way to my mother in the flesh, cooking spoon in hand, like an improvised conductor's baton to encourage my teacher to keep playing.

"Get out," I hissed.

We were alone then, the three of us—Liliana, me, and Chopin, whose first name I never asked for; during the few minutes that my teacher played, I learned everything about him that I would ever need to know.

"That's a nocturne," Liliana said when she was done.

I opened my eyes and felt a heat rise to my cheeks that I can still feel today.

"Oh," I said.

"Do you want to try a few bars?"

"It looks so different from Bach."

"Don't be afraid. I'll help you."

*

It was only natural that I would fall in love, years later, with someone I thought loved Chopin the way Liliana had taught me to love him. Anatol was more than a foreign accent in fine clothes, but those were the two things I noticed about him first, living in a small town with sidewalks stained by chewing tobacco and baseball hats strung like salamis out of nearly every shop window. The third thing I noticed was the disposable Starbucks cup in his hands. Anatol cradled it like the finest French porcelain, raising it to his lips and sipping so slowly, it was a wonder the coffee did not evaporate before reaching his mouth. When I tried to mimic his movements, he was the first to offer me a napkin.

"Thanks," I said, immediately regretting the choice of that unsophisticated word. "Thank you very much."

As we mopped up the mess together, I could already see into the future, though not far enough to have stopped myself from going downtown and making that fated left turn toward the coffee shop.

"I also have this." He reached into his pocket and pulled out a handkerchief.

"Incredible," I said. "Do you have a pocket watch too?"

"Of course," he said, and pulled that out as well. "But these are functional items, not props. Look." Unfolding the handkerchief, he leaned over and wiped a single drop of coffee from the back of my hand.

I was twenty-five then, going on fifteen. I had not thought of my piano teacher in years, and the lid of the piano in my parents' living room stayed closed, even when I came home to visit.

"I am Anatol," the delightful man said. He pronounced his name with a confidence that should have turned heads, but a quick glance around the room reminded me that newness is not always prized in a place that never changes. Mine was the only pounding heart in the entire city; I was sure of that. We shook hands, and Anatol's dark eyes reflected the warmth that flowed freely from his fingers into mine.

Later, my mother would insist that his dress shirts, which I had always praised, were of the non-iron polyester variety, and what more needed to be said? But I knew better, that Anatol worked out every wrinkle himself, until the smoothness of the fabric matched that of the skin against which it rested, and against which I too would come to rest for the next few short months. When, in response to a question about his origins, he explained that he was a citizen of the world, a window into the world I had been living in was suddenly wrenched open, and I saw it for the smallness that it was, followed by the bigness that it was about to become. As if someone else had put the question into my mouth, I asked Anatol if he liked Chopin.

*

The tiny college in the town where we lived offered concerts. Anatol invited me to every one. We always made love afterward, his gelled black hair shedding onto my bedsheets and staying there for weeks, because who washes bedsheets before the age of thirty? He wanted to know everything about me, especially about the Jewish part of me, something I had taken for granted we shared, since his foreignness felt so familiar. I was happy to talk, and chatted away, surprising myself with stories from my grandmother's shtetl—the Ukrainian peasant bands that roamed through it; clashes between the Reds and the Whites; the bullet lodged in Bubbe's wrist during the Russo-Japanese War; fleeing for America with a feather bed and two pillows; a small room above a grocery store on Eighth Street in Philadelphia. Anatol listened attentively and stroked my wrist when I held it up to show where the scar had been. When I finished, he closed his eyes and let it all sink in.

"I am sure your grandmother brought more than a feather bed with her," he said when he opened his eyes again.

"Two pillows," I reminded him.

"She must have been a very beautiful woman."

"She had a deep dimple on her chin."

"A very cultured woman," Anatol said. "A lover of music, just like you."

"My grandfather played the accordion."

"And of art, I'm sure."

We went to an exhibit of birch-bark baskets at the local museum. I was grateful that the room was small, and guessed we would be free again in about five minutes, the length of time I usually spent at exhibits if I didn't take a bathroom break. But Anatol had other plans, and we walked round and round the room as if we were stuck in a continuous loop, and with no screen to project ourselves onto. Finally he pointed to one of the baskets and said, "You see how the rim on this one is protected? By sewing on a metal band. Birch bark is fragile, and splits very easily."

I nodded. "Can we do that now?"

"What?"

"Split?"

Anatol smiled. "But we just arrived."

"To this basket, yes. But there were three hundred others before it."

Staring sympathetically at the high heels I had exchanged my tennis shoes for (the first of many alterations I would make for Anatol), he offered me his arm and led me gracefully toward the exit. "Have you ever seen the body paintings done by the Kwakiutl Indians?" he asked.

"No," I said.

We were outside again, squinting at each other in the sunshine and waiting for the free trolley to come and whisk us away.

"They are very beautiful and usually represent a bear, with dark spirals encircling the buttocks for the hip joints, and more spirals on the leg to suggest a tail. Come, let us go back to your place and I will paint your body like a bear."

If there had ever been a doubt before then, in that instant I was Anatol's.

"You'll paint a bear on my body?" I repeated, making sure I understood right so that I could will my neck hairs to stand even higher on end.

"Over every inch of it," Anatol confirmed.

*

My mother was her usual clueless self when I called. "Why do you keep going on about Bubbe, may she rest in peace?" she said when I asked whether she could recall the motif on Bubbe's kiddush cup, and how many generations back she'd received it.

"Anatol loves Bubbe," I explained.

"Does he not know what 'may she rest in peace' means?"

"He loves history," I said. "I told him about the village scene inscribed on the cup, and he dated it all the way back to the tsar, without even knowing which village."

I'm pretty sure my mother was charmed. "When can we meet him?" she asked.

I was lying in my bed, studying the prints left behind by Anatol's bear. The sheets were saturated with fourteen colors of edible paint, but we had remembered to wash the paintbrushes for future use.

"Probably never," I said. "But I've stopped biting my fingernails, and I'm going for my first manicure tomorrow. I'll send you a picture."

"Of *him*," my mother said.

"We each have a mole in the exact same place on our right cheeks."

My mother was one step ahead of me. "Don't do it," she implored. "Sweetie, if you pluck that hair, ten will take its place. Believe me, I know."

"Too late," I said. "I'll send you a picture."

*

If Anatol had heeded my warning at the restaurant, he would not have required my help getting home on the night of his first Caesar salad. It was going on nine o'clock and the kitchen was about to close, a fact that Anatol could not fathom, just as he had refused to believe that the hummus at a different restaurant a few days earlier was thickened with peanut butter.

"Don't be fooled by the name," I warned him. "Look, they didn't even capitalize the *C*. Maybe you should order the chicken wings?"

Anatol looked, then closed the menu. "Crossing the Rubicon doesn't have to be hard. The Caesar salad, please," he said to Kim, our server, who had pledged to take care of us that night.

He was so resistant to turning on a light in his apartment that it was the first thing I did after finding him a bucket to barf in. We had made love in his bed only once before, and that time too he had demanded darkness. At my place he was always looking for candlesticks.

If I had understood a single thing about Anatol, well, I might never have fallen for him in the first place. It was a shame someone with so aesthetic an eye left his walls in such a sorry state; the nail holes and peeling paint did precious little to spruce up what could have been a home, rather than a room with a bucket to barf in.

"Anatol? You OK in there?"

Sitting on a couch was not an option, and the wicker chair in the corner evoked those awful baskets, so I made myself comfortable on the floor and flipped through a few of the hundred or so art books that were bookmarked in a million places, all with fragments of Starbucks napkins. Luckily, no scissors lay nearby, or I would have been more than a little tempted to cut out the first twenty pages of *From the Renaissance to Romanticism* and tape them to the walls.

When Anatol emerged from the bathroom, he looked ready to go back to the restaurant and order another salad. Flipping off the light switch, he crouched down beside me, his mouth minty. He was wearing a new braided leather belt he had taught me how to remove with my teeth.

"Can I sleep here tonight?" I asked. "To help you finally move in?"

"For a man, a house is less a place he enters than a place he comes out of," he said, turning his head just as I was taking aim for his lips. "Come, let's get some ice cream."

Even without ice cream, I would have liked being in love. It was so easy to settle into a state of blissfulness and miss all the signals that should have sent me running back to school to learn what human beings are made of; I didn't know then that pain is felt more strongly than pleasure. Still, even if someone had stopped me in the street and warned me of what was to come, I would have shaken my head and replied, *Pain? How do you spell that?*

One evening, Anatol spoke for ten straight minutes about my hair: the weight of it like gold under his fingers; its thickness a forest he could lose himself in; the springiness of my curls reminiscent of an exhibit of Egyptian coil bracelets he'd attended in Cairo itself. I listened and waited for him to move on to another part of my body, preferably one with nerve endings. But just as suddenly as he had started, he stopped talking and lowered his eyes to the floor.

"I like your hair too," I offered.

"It is disgusting," Anatol said.

"Not at all. But if you want to switch to mousse, I just bought a new bottle."

"And look at your apartment. The walls would be better off bare, like mine, than with what you have disgraced them with."

I followed his eyes toward two lovers floating behind a vase of flowers. "You said you loved Chagall."

"A poster from a gift shop," Anatol spit.

"Not at all," I said. I could clear up this misunderstanding as quickly as it had come between us, out of the blue, without warning, like a parachutist with the wrong coordinates landing in my living room. "Bubbe gave it to me for my bat mitzvah. Would you like to see some pictures from the party?"

Anatol stood up, all six finely pressed feet of him. "I have seen enough," he said. He left then, and didn't come back later that evening, as I was sure he would, or the following morning, as fate should have demanded.

I tried easing the pain of Anatol's absence in so many ways: by standing outside in the rain, by sleeping for twenty hours straight, by cutting multiple locks of my hair to press between the pages of a Hallmark card. Whatever I did only made me miss him more, especially sitting alone at Starbucks and seeing it for the unmagical place that it was, each table a trip to nowhere. The paper cup in front of me said, "DRINK ME" in big letters, but its meaning was lost on me entirely, and my mouth stayed closed.

One night, I heard a voice calling me from far away, and when I leaned in to listen, it was my mother, telling me to take myself out of that town.

I'll be there tomorrow, I whispered.

You'll watch the clock—I know you—and tomorrow will never come, my mother whispered back.

I took the first train toward my childhood home. The windows of the Amtrak were sealed shut, but I could feel a breeze blow through my flat-ironed hair, the sensation growing stronger the farther south we traveled. At the halfway point, the train stopped to change engines, and the woman sitting next to me, a diabetic with several missing toes, stood up to stretch her legs.

"You are one skinny thing," she observed, eyeing me from this new angle.

At these words, an utter exhaustion enveloped me, so heavy and unyielding, I didn't feel skinny at all.

"My hair." I motioned to my siliconized scalp and the hardened strands that hung from it like icicles after a deep freeze. "It's usually different—big, with a life of its own. I needed to tame it for a while."

The woman considered my excuse, then plopped back down onto her seat and resumed drinking her bottle of soda. "Your mama needs to fatten you up," she said.

My mother had timed my arrival perfectly, or maybe she had simply been standing outside on the porch for hours in anticipation of it. She struck me as beautiful, someone who would never need a bear painted on her body for it to come to life. It was hot outside, but she was wearing multiple layers of clothing, including a pair of long johns under her pants, which she had done for as long as I could remember, as if in homage to our desert ancestors.

"The soup is ready," my mother said. She took me by the hand and led me inside.

*

It is difficult to eat soup without making a sound, but we managed to do so, as if my mother's mouth and mine were one. After a few spoonfuls, our mouths assumed a different shape, rendering the spoon superfluous, and we both began to cry.

"What did this man do to you?" my mother asked, pushing her plate away.

"He showed me the world," I sobbed.

"Like hell he did," my mother said. "The world is beautiful."

A breeze blew through a window in the living room, and out of the corner of my eye I saw a page flutter from an open book on the piano stand, the same page that always fluttered when I came to visit, quietly calling for someone to take notice.

"OK," I said.

But the piano bench reminded me of all the restaurant booths I had shared with Anatol, and then of the seat on the train that had taken me far away from Anatol. I sat for a few minutes waiting for something to happen and then got up to cry again, a pattern that repeated itself over the next half hour, until my mother blocked my path to the bathroom and placed a book with a hideous green cover in my hand.

"Remember this?" she said.

"Barely," I sniffled.

"Open it," my mother instructed.

And there was that lovely name, written neatly in pencil on the inside. A name I hadn't thought about in years, but that suddenly meant more to me than Chopin and Bach combined. How could that be?

"Liliana," I whispered.

I placed my fingers on the piano keys and played.

Vignette of the North

Simona didn't need to study painting to know that every Sunday between seven o'clock and noon she was in the presence of a great artist. She could feel it from her tomato stall, watching the painter work in bold, broad strokes. His specialty was landscapes—mountains, hills, valleys, trees, rocks, bridges, and winding roads; Simona had noted them all. Sometimes he added water scenes. For a reflection or a ripple he needed only to push and lift with a pastel stick, and there it was.

One morning Simona discovered her very own vegetables taking shape on the painter's easel and could not hide her delight. She had been walking by *Vignette of the North*, her favorite picture—five rings of water spreading out under a school of bright, leaping fish—when she noticed a pyramid of tomatoes materializing from under his brush. Simona went back to her seat, but fixed her eyes on the canvas as more of the picture fell into place. Although there were other vegetable stands at the farmer's market, she found the likeness too great for it to be anything but her stall. The only thing missing from the scene was her in it, fishing for change from the pocket of her apron. It could hold ten dollars in quarters alone.

Hesitantly Simona approached the painter, who was bent over a cardboard box. "Excuse me," she said.

The painter pulled the box closer to him, as if

protecting a secret. "Later, later," he said, without looking up.

Simona stepped back. "Of course," she apologized, and quickly returned to her stall.

At the end of the day Simona watched as her neighbors lifted their remaining goods—a few crates of corn, some baskets of muffins, three oversize coolers of Pete's Hot Pepper Gelato—onto the backs of pickup trucks and hauled them away. Her tomatoes had gotten off to a good start in the early morning, when the older crowd came looking for the freshest vegetables to can for the winter. She had never learned to can; the tomatoes she took home usually ended up in soups and sauces, or sometimes in the freezer in the form of ice cubes, which she sucked on late at night while watching television or mending a shirt. If she forgot to refreeze the tray, the ice cubes would turn to sauce again, and she would stir them into a bowl of spaghetti the following day and have them for lunch.

The painter had removed a new work to show to a young couple. "You're looking at the Pripet Marshes, which were a work in progress until last night," he explained, placing it on his easel. "That's when I realized the Russian army, which has always defended the Marshes from European invaders, could hold them no longer, because I had captured them myself, right here." He flicked a finger against the canvas. "The missing whiskers from each of the four cattails represent the four nations throughout history that attempted—and failed—to take the Marshes, including the Swedes, with whom I am said to share some blood."

After the couple left, Simona once more approached the painter, who appeared eager to start a new conversation. She was not sure that he wanted to speak to her in particular, just that he wanted to speak. His mouth, partly hidden by an ample beard, hung half-open, as if in preparation to complete a sentence it had started the day before. The rest of his face relied on a pair of pale blue eyes, which blinked in slow intervals and only after finding an object to settle on. Eventually they settled on Simona.

"Congratulations on capturing the Marshes," she said. "Now all you need to do is sell them."

The painter pressed his palms against the table of his stall and leaned forward. "From your mouth to God's ears," he said. Carefully he stepped back to consider his painting from the proper perspective. "It's a problem."

"What's a problem?"

"The Marshes. Wetlands never sell well. People want to look at either dry or wet, but not swampy. In my next water scene I'll have two century-old clippers racing each other home with cargo from China and Australia. The waves will come crashing right into the face of the client."

Simona nodded in approval. "I've never seen you work with waves." She pictured the ripples in her favorite piece gathering momentum, the fish riding the water like surfers in the sea. "But I did see you painting my vegetable stand, and I hope you'll let me make you an offer once you've put me in it." She paused, then added, "Have you sold *Vignette of the North* yet?"

The painter reached for a paper bag under the table. He did not seem surprised by Simona's familiarity with his portfolio and stood up bearing a powdered-sugar croissant between his teeth. "*Vignette of the North* I have not sold," he said gravely. "*Vignette of the Northeast* I have not sold. Behind the palm trees in *Vignette of the South* looms an overcast sky in lavender gray that makes me cry every time I look at it."

Simona watched the croissant disappear into the painter's mouth and felt her face flush. She remembered the sky in *Vignette of the South*, the colors cast with the heel of a hand. It was the first of his landscapes she had observed in the making, a dozen flicks of the wrist for every palm frond, and since then she'd made it a point every week to set up her stall early, determined not to miss a stroke.

"Lavender gray sounds nice," she said, wanting to offer some encouragement. "Almost as nice as the colors you've chosen to paint my stall."

The painter was drinking a bottle of water now, and wincing as the cold liquid hit his teeth. "The last dentist I went to had a better eye than me," he said. "He saw a whole menagerie of savage animals feeding on my gums. The farther back he looked, the more species he saw."

"That's quite a vivid description."

"You should have seen the bill."

A group of sparrows were gathered around the stall where a Mennonite family had sold cinnamon buns, but the rest of the market aisles were empty now. Simona stared at a crumb that had settled on the painter's beard and wished it away. As the object of artistic inspiration, she felt almost entitled to brush it off herself. "If you'd like," she proposed as he gathered his things, "we could have dinner, and then recreate my stall in my living room. You could finish your picture there, without all the distractions of the market. It will look just like the real thing, and I'm a very good cook."

Tossing the empty water bottle into an abandoned crate, the painter stuck a finger in his mouth and began to massage his gums. "For an artist, only what is imagined is real," he replied, slurring his words a little.

Simona had no trouble understanding him. "Yes," she said, picturing herself in her living room, tilting her head toward the angle of the painter's brush. "I know exactly what you mean."

*

The painter arrived promptly at seven o'clock, a long, narrow duffel bag slung over his shoulder, just as Simona was arranging a bunch of daisies in a vase. Two cast iron pots sat simmering on the stove and the table had been set since early afternoon, a tall-stemmed glass to the right of each plate for the wine she hoped the painter would bring. Simona hung up the painter's coat and offered him two chairs in the living room, one for his person and the other for the parcel in his arms—*Vignette of the North,* which she would mount in an oak frame above the fireplace once they agreed on a price.

The painter pushed the two chairs together and laid the parcel flat across them. "Bubble wrap is for the devil," he said, jiggling the chairs for sturdiness. "When I die, they can wrap my body in it."

Simona pulled out a third chair for him in the dining room, and the two sat down for dinner. "Have you been painting for a long time?" she asked, pouring ice water into the painter's wineglass. "It took me ages to understand how the flesh of a tomato is formed."

"My first painting was a portrait of my grandfather's dead body on his hospital bed. The color of his skin changed three times in forty-five minutes."

Simona brought her napkin to her lips and held it there. "I've never been anyone's muse before," she said.

The painter plucked a trio of basil leaves from the tomato salad in front of him and pushed them to the side of his plate. "Eskimos eat every part of the seal they catch except the bladder and bones. Those they throw back into the sea, fearing the spirit of the seal will haunt them if they don't."

Simona stared for a moment, disappointed but not offended. She said, "I prefer unseasoned vegetables myself, just sliced, with a little lemon juice and olive oil. But there's nothing like fresh basil from the garden."

After dinner, they went out back to look at a patch of zucchini that had come under attack by slugs the night before. It was the third such incident that month, after light rains had driven the creatures out of the compost heap and onto Simona's plants, and it was the first time they had chewed their way down from the tops of the vegetables, rather than from the bottoms up.

At the sight of the damage, Simona turned off her flashlight and led the painter through the rest of the patch in darkness, stopping every few feet to feel for a zucchini intact enough to pick.

"I should have changed into my work clothes before coming out here," she said, and flicked a wet leaf from her flashlight. "But the red in this dress will complement the tomatoes in your picture so nicely."

Trailing Simona by several feet, the painter clasped his hands behind his back and stared up at the sky. "One hour before sunset, a clear sky is bathed in a violet white. And in the shadows it will give off an orange gray."

"How interesting," replied Simona. "I've often wondered what makes evening colors stronger."

The painter waited for her at the end of a row. "The dust in the air," he replied.

With a half-full bucket of zucchini, Simona and the painter went back inside. In the living room Simona pulled a thin blanket from a La-Z-Boy recliner and sat down. "Is this where you want me?" She popped up the footrest and stretched out her legs. "I can sit here for hours without moving a muscle."

While she waited, the painter paced up and down before the chairs, where *Vignette of the North* still lay, bound in its protective plastic. It was a strange sight for Simona, watching someone she was used to seeing confined to a few feet suddenly expand his territory to a whole room. A strange sight, but not an unpleasant one.

Against the wall stood a fern in a ceramic pot. The painter approached the plant and swiped at it with the back of his hand, sending errant leaves spiraling to the ground. "Is this a fern?" he asked.

"Yes," said Simona from her chair.

"I would never trust myself to paint a plant that existed millions of years before the first flower." He turned on his heels and resumed pacing. "If you want to be in my picture, you'll have to hang it in another room."

The painter finally unpacked his supplies. The coolness of his movements gave the impression of someone who had come to fix a leaky pipe or tune a piano. When he leaned over, a faint smell of burned toast filled the air.

After removing a thin brush from his lunch bag, the painter dipped it into a bottle of water. "Usually, the longer a painter looks at his easel, the less he sees. But if I so much as bend down to tie my shoe while I am working, the image before my eyes will have vanished by the time I stand up again."

Simona stared at the painter's shoes and imagined a pair of invisible hands lifting her from the chair and carrying her off to a remote corner of his consciousness. "Would you like to take off your shoes?" she suggested.

For the next hour the painter worked, lowering his brush only to switch colors or scratch an itch. When he got hungry he pulled a pickle from a paper bag, feeding himself in sloppy bites with a free hand. Simona tried to concentrate on being painted with the same intensity the painter exhibited in painting. When his eyes widened, she widened hers; when a patch of perspiration appeared at his brow, she let her head hang back toward the open window in the room. She thought of her tomatoes lined up at the stall, some perfectly round, some egg-shaped or elongated, some indented, wobbly, or bruised, and regretted that the only way to integrate them was to let them liquefy in a pot of onions and garlic.

By ten o'clock, the painting was finished. Kicking in

the footrest, Simona stood up from her chair and hurried to the bathroom. When she returned, the painter had taken her place in the recliner and sat with closed eyes, his lids fluttering as if trying to fight off sleep.

Simona took three steps toward the easel, then stopped with another three to go. "Can I look?" she asked.

The painter opened his eyes. "You can look. You can like. You can even buy," he said.

For a moment, Simona was tempted to run back to the bathroom and take a peek at herself in the mirror. She was not unattractive; her forehead was smooth and broad, compensating, perhaps, for a nose a little too narrow. Her cheekbones were high and her ears small and fleshy, the lobes impressively long for having never been pierced. A small scratch to her cornea acquired during a high school camping trip still caused a periodic reddening of her right eye. But in most light, it was barely detectable.

Taking a deep breath, she faced the finished work. Splayed out on the canvas before her, in varying shades of yellow, was an enormous ear of corn, its brown tassels hanging like limp locks of hair. Behind the corn stood rows of melon vines, and behind them, a dwarfed windmill surrounded by clusters of oak trees and sand hills. The sky was white, suggesting clear atmospheric conditions and a midafternoon hour. Dark green, the only other color in the painting, carried the curved tips of the corn leaves and settled along the edges of the stalk.

Simona stared hard at the painting. Her eyes darted in every direction, trying to find a break in the landscape where her image would suddenly appear, bright and forceful, like a sliver of sun. She studied the clump of trees and the rows of vines. She looked beyond the windmill and the distant sand hills to a spot on the easel that had been speckled black. Finally she turned away from the canvas.

"Why corn?" she asked politely.

The painter nodded. "I remembered too late that it should have been tomatoes," he said. "But if you look carefully at the base of the stalk, you'll see a ring of striped yellow-headed larvae, which feed on corn and tomatoes alike. I didn't put them in there for the fun of it."

Simona could summon the image of an earworm in her sleep, its little round head boring holes the size of Q-tips into the flesh of her tomatoes. She quickly found them on the canvas, long, tapered cylinders stuck to the cornstalk like grains of rice to a pot. With a fingernail, she scraped at the wet picture until one of the worms disappeared. "They're disgusting," she said, holding up her finger. "Even worse than slugs."

At these words, the painter jumped up from the recliner and began collapsing his easel. "To complete my painting of the tomato stall, I need to find the right face," he explained. "If you want to be in a picture, you'll have to wait until I do a winter scene, set somewhere high in the mountains."

"Do I have a long forehead?" Simona asked.

The painter shrugged.

"But it's my stall you're painting," she reminded him. "Who else belongs in it if not me?"

Slouching from the weight of his supplies, the painter moved toward the door. "I'll know that by next week," he said.

*

On the last day of the farmer's market Simona lay in bed longer than usual and waited for the sun to rise, knowing that when it crept through her window she would have to double her efforts if she wanted to set up her stall on time. She was not sure she did; only six crates of tomatoes sat on the back porch, a far cry from the dozen she averaged at the height of the season. Even her own supply was running low, the green of spinach starting to replace the red that had dominated her refrigerator for the last three months. Soon she would have to start shopping at the supermarket again.

Simona pulled into her parking spot at the market and began setting up her wares. Though it was still early, a number of people were waiting in front of her stall, many watching with interest as she unfolded a green lawn chair from the back of her truck and sat down. She was even more surprised when these same people passed her produce by to stand in line at the next stall, where the painter sat animatedly at his easel, waving his paintbrush through the air.

"Would all the men please step aside," Simona heard him request of the growing crowd. "I won't consider anyone with a bilious complexion, who digests badly, sleeps little, and doesn't take his meals at proper hours. This applies to most men over the age of thirty."

Standing on tiptoe, Simona peered over the group's heads to get a better view of the painter's easel. Propped against it she saw her tomato stall, unfinished as before, but with a conspicuously vacant green lawn chair sketched in. She sat down again and waited for her customers to arrive.

When the line at the painter's stall had dwindled to two college-age girls in fleece jogging suits, Simona left her tomatoes and walked over to join them.

"You're wasting my time," the painter was saying impatiently, swatting the taller girl's ponytail. "Anyone with hair as thin as yours is predisposed to all kinds of accidents, and in some cases a violent death. That's exactly the wrong kind of karma for my picture."

Simona waited for the joggers to leave, then stepped into the space they had eagerly abandoned. "None of the people you rejected today will ever buy a tomato from me again," she said.

An old kerchiefed woman pulled a collapsible cart past the stall. She stopped at the end of the table, then backed up to squint at the sign the painter had erected that morning.

"You want only face, or also legs?" the woman asked, lifting the hem of her skirt to reveal a network of thick blue veins. "Legs no good. Face all right."

"No face, and no legs." The painter tossed a shirt over the easel. "Finished. For sale."

"No face?" Simona repeated.

"No face, no frame. Like a wide expanse of sea contained by a single fisherman in a fishing boat."

"That sounds like one of your paintings."

The painter shook his head, bit down on a knuckle, and winced. "With gums as inflamed as mine, I can only think of fire, not water."

A gray cloud hovering over the market swallowed the sky's last patch of blue and released a spray of warm, feathery rain into the air. Simona wondered if these were the painter's parting words, and did not know what hers should be. Generally she was good at responding to other people's pain. When her neighbor's dog was hit by a car, she'd brought over a vegetarian lasagna large enough to last a week. And when one of her customers confided that her husband had run off with another woman, Simona had added a complimentary box of cucumbers to her tomatoes.

But at the thought of the painter's gums, Simona remained unmoved. Standing silently before him, she thought of the red dress she had worn for the sitting, hanging in her closet like a scarecrow in a field.

"If you need a dentist, Dr. Arthur Spano is excellent," she finally said. She approached the painting of her stall one more time and pulled the shirt from the canvas. The lawn chair was still empty. "They cater to cowards," she added.

*

For the next two weeks it rained steadily. Simona spent her mornings indoors at the Garden Center filling bags with potting soil, while outside in her own garden streams of water were beginning to carve gullies and valleys into the foundation of her soil. When, at the end of the second week, the sky finally started to clear, she brought home a rattlesnake fern wrapped in newspaper, its young leaves still wound up into coils, and placed it on her kitchen windowsill in homage to the sunlight that had slunk its way through the thinning clouds.

On her way to the Garden Center each morning, Simona passed the Professional Services Building, a gray somber structure where, in Dr. Spano's office a year earlier, she had read an article about a Polish jam factory caught manufacturing tiny plastic pellets for its famous Radjinicz Raspberry Preserves. At the stoplight closest to the dentist's office, Simona would sometimes crane her neck out the car window to get a glimpse of the patients entering and exiting the narrow wooden door. When she spotted a beard, she would crane her neck a little farther; when the path leading up to the entrance was empty, she would wait impatiently for someone to appear before the light turned green. Soon the game she had invented for herself grew tiresome, and one morning she put an end to it by swinging into the parking lot to set up an appointment for a cleaning.

The receptionist was on the phone when she walked in. Picking up an issue of *Gourmet,* Simona sat down and tried to commit to memory a recipe for mushroom moussaka, cutting the yield of eight servings in half to four, and then again in half to two. When the receptionist was off the phone, Simona scheduled an appointment for two weeks before Christmas, on the same day she was due to have a mole removed in the office next door.

"That's two presents I don't have to wrap," she said, writing down the date on a slip of paper.

On her way out Simona stopped in the bathroom, on whose door a hand-painted sign read, "We cater to cowards." Before she sat down on the toilet she looked in the mirror and plucked a thick black hair that had begun to sprout from the mole on her cheek.

Her face pressing toward the glass, Simona suddenly felt her urge to urinate disappear like the hair she had just washed down the drain. Reflected in the mirror she saw her tomato stall, its contents reversely arranged, hanging in a gilded frame above the toilet. She turned around to look again, and the image became even bolder. There, in the center of the picture, sitting comfortably in Simona's lawn chair, with his legs stretched out like a cat waking from a nap, was the painter.

Simona returned to the waiting room and waited for the receptionist to finish with a patient. Then she asked, "Is that picture in the bathroom for sale?"

"That one's not. Dr. Spano got it from a patient who couldn't pay. But if you go down to the X-ray room at the end of the hall, all those are," the receptionist said. "Dr. Spano's wife's been at it for years."

Simona did not follow the receptionist's directions. Instead she went back to the bathroom and stood in front of the mirror with the lights off. For a moment she thought she had returned to snatch the painting off the wall and claim it as her own. It would not have lasted long in her possession; she would have donated it to charity or used it for firewood. But the longer she stood in the dark, the more convinced she became that the proper place for such a painting was where it now hung, above a toilet in a dentist's office, far from the walls of a museum or the warmth of a private home.

Turning on the faucet, Simona recalled *Vignette of the North* covered in bubble wrap and imagined the leaping fish inside lying inertly on their backs, their life source dried up. She thought of the dishes she had washed after her evening with the painter, the side of his plate scattered with an array of rejected seasonings, and of the painter's muddy footprints on her carpet, which he had remarked he would not charge her for. As the water continued to flow down the drain, Simona allowed herself a final look at the painting, then quickly walked over to the light switch and turned it on.

There, under the watchful eye of the painter, she sat down on the toilet and peed.

FLOATING ON WATER

Abby is a woman, and I am a woman. To prove we are friends she often sleeps on my couch with her toenails digging into the soft leather. In the morning I find her sprawled out like a drunkard, one half of her body sagging toward the floor, the other half stuck to the couch in stubborn repose. There is never any warning before she arrives; I may open the door to check for the mail and find her walking up the steps, or a phone call may inform me that her train has pulled into the station ten minutes early and that a cab will take her the rest of the way. To prepare for her visits I usually manage to take quick inventory of my kitchen and stow away anything that is imported, especially the Viennese marzipan hearts that I like to curl up with when I've had a bad day. The rest I leave to Abby's disposal, knowing I will be the better for it after she has gone.

When Abby comes to visit, all we do is eat. If we go out and split the bill, I end up paying for three times the amount of food that is in my stomach. Usually Abby pays for dinner, and I treat for dessert. But this can be costly too.

Abby is a woman, and I am a woman. It could be argued that Abby is more of a woman than I am. Wherever she goes she finds men to love her—or to make love to her—even if she has to go far to find them. Her last trip took her to Hong Kong and Shanghai. As a parting gift her tour guide presented her with a porcelain box engraved with a man and a woman copulating, penis and vagina fully exposed. I am as slender as a flower; bracelets will slide onto my wrists without any effort. But I have not been loved by a man in over a year.

The last time Abby visited she had been seeing a Moroccan, not in Morocco but in New York, where she lives. We were sitting in an Indian restaurant sharing a vegetarian *thali*; Abby was dressed in a skirt that revealed the width of her thighs and gave off a scent of baby powder whenever she shifted position. When the waiter came to refill our water glasses, Abby fished out a piece of ice with her lips and munched on it like a piece of hard candy. "Shakir won't kiss me," she said, leaning forward to keep it private. "He'll sleep with me, but he won't kiss me. Isn't that fucked?"

I stared at Abby's lips while she spoke. "You mean he won't initiate a kiss, or he won't return one?"

She crunched down on another cube. "He actually told me, 'No kissing,'" she explained. "He says that in Morocco kissing is reserved for love. I told him that in America, fucking without kissing is called date rape."

The waiter walked by, and I flagged him down for more ice. "So it sounds like you have a deal," I said, trying to put a positive spin on the situation. I thought of the last man I dated, a man who craved closeness like a baby in its mother's arms. After every physical encounter he thanked me bashfully, feeling unworthy of my affection. I finally told him that thanking me *made* him unworthy, and he apologized for the rest of the evening, making himself even less worthy than before.

"Deal, my ass; I love to kiss. But he's a good cook." As though to demonstrate, Abby plunged a spoon into a bowl of saag paneer and delivered it to her mouth.

"He cooks for you?"

"He cooks for himself," Abby said. "I smell it on his clothing, the bastard. Lamb, apricots, cinnamon everywhere. I'm going to invite myself over soon."

*

Two days after Abby left, I went on a walk with my friend Prema. We sat on a bench in a dog park and watched the grass around us get trampled and shit on by canines staking out their territory. I was still thinking about Abby, still puzzling over why her presence seemed to cast a shadow in my apartment. "Have you ever heard of a tree in India," I asked Prema, who was from India, "that produces gorgeous orange blossoms but only if kicked by a beautiful woman?"

Prema looked up at the towering maple above us and shook her head. "We could use a few of those here," she said, poking at the urine-stained trunk with a stick.

Sometimes, at unexpected moments like this one, Abby's face will appear before my eyes and I will find myself studying it, looking desperately for a well-formed nose or long lashes or a fair complexion to make up for all those extra pounds. "One of the waiters at Maharajah told me about the tree when I was eating there with a friend," I explained. "But it was my friend he was speaking to, who is supremely overweight."

"I'm sure she took it as a compliment," Prema said,

pulling her long black hair into a ponytail. "If nothing else, trees are great for hiding behind."

Two golden retrievers ran by, stirring up a cloud of dust by our feet. Though it was still early the sky was starting to darken, separating itself from the sun that had filled it like yolk in an egg. I thought of Abby hiding behind an umbrella, her face obscured but the legs below her miniskirt exposed, and I knew that something about the image didn't work, that Abby never hid. When the first drop of rain fell, Prema and I got up from the bench and started for home. The two golden retrievers followed us as far as the park entrance, then turned around and trotted off in the opposite direction, as though they had just remembered where they were and what they had come to do.

*

At work, a man began taking his coffee breaks at my cubicle. He would stand near my right elbow with his steaming mug raised; through the vapors he appeared a benevolent phantom trying to rouse me from a stupor I had been in for too long. We went to the movies and out to dinner, then for coffee, a stroll through town, a stop at CVS for stamps, and back to Starbucks for a refill. Three miles at least, all told. At the end of the evening David and I stood outside the coffee shop exhausted, and I listened to him wonder whether we had tried to pack too many things into our first date. "I really didn't need these stamps," he said, taking two books of classic-car stamps out of his back pocket and offering me one of them. "And outside of work I'm not much of a coffee drinker."

"Don't apologize, I had a good time." Without letting my fingers wander, I pushed the stamps back into David's pocket and leaned against the brick wall of the Starbucks, trying to gauge the level of attraction I felt toward a man I had seen probably a hundred times but barely noticed. Under the romantic glow of the street lamp we must have appeared as two young lovers loath to part, the beating of our hearts, as the last sips of latte entered our bloodstreams, audible to anyone walking by. For a while we just stood there absorbing the activity around us like two apprentices learning a trade. When a bus pulled up to the curb and opened its doors, David turned to me and said, "Should we get on?" I checked my pockets for change and followed him up the steps. For three complete loops we sat at the very front, in seats reserved for the elderly or disabled, and nobody asked us to move.

At work I waited for a sign—a quick kiss in the kitchen, flowers sent to my cubicle, a romantic e-mail written on the job in strict violation of company rules. I thought of David as he sat one room over filing papers and recording data and tried to wish away all the awkwardness between us by anticipating the moment when our relationship would become intimate, all the words we had exchanged trying to get to know each other broken down into their most primal elements. During coffee breaks David stood next to me and struck up conversations with complete strangers, regaling them with stories of summers spent on farms in Georgia and his mother's recipe for homemade fertilizer. I wanted to believe the energy he expended was for my benefit and that communication through a third party was the best way for him to convey information he felt I needed to know. Over the course of three days I heard him confide to as many people that his true calling in life was to become a professional gardener.

*

I dreamed I was fat. In my dream Prema and I were back at the park, watching the dogs and discussing transmigration. "Look at me," I said, holding out a flabby arm. "I'm becoming someone else."

Prema disagreed. "It's your soul sending you a sign that you've lived a righteous life," she said.

When I woke up I spent an hour online, learning that when a soul is worthy it becomes food before passing to a new abode. First it goes to paradise, then to the moon. From the moon it passes to the air and descends to the earth again in the form of a fruit or a vegetable. I called Prema and asked her to explain it to me, to tell me which fruit and which vegetable, and whether she thought I had gained weight in the last few weeks. "Transmigration is about deeds, not diets," she said wisely. "It's about the actions of one life affecting the next."

"Either this guy I'm seeing is a complete loser, or I am," I said, trying to interpret the dream for myself. "Which do you think it is?"

"Have you lived a life of sacrifice and charity?" Prema pressed.

Standing in line at CVS, David had told me that his mother's dream for him was that he become a carpenter. "That's probably how I ended up behind a desk, which isn't even real wood," he theorized bitterly.

"I'll invite him over," I promised Prema.

*

On our second date, David appeared at the threshold of my apartment with a six-pack of beer in his hands and said, "Hey," before stepping inside. "Hey," I returned reluctantly, fearful of being thought one of the guys and not the woman I had just given cautious approval to a minute before in the bathroom mirror. "Come in," I said, relieving him of his gift. "I was just about to open a bottle of wine."

Almost immediately we took refuge in another movie. From my peripheral vision I observed David as we lay sprawled out on my futon, our eyes keeping pace with the images racing across the screen. When a love scene commenced he started to stir, the upper part of his body shifting uneasily as if trying to slow down the forces rapidly filling his lower half. I sensed what was to come and braced myself for it. I had pictured taking it slow, not to savor the experience but to ensure that the steps I had taken to make it my own did not go unnoticed: the rose water in my hair, the sage oil worked into my skin, the Chinese silk undergarments I kept wrapped in lemongrass on the top shelf of a small cedar closet. Within two minutes David was on top of me, spurred into action by the sex on-screen and the accessibility of it right next to him. The sounds in the room were rapid and resolute, like a series of shots fired from a gun, and they did not come from me.

Afterward he popped open a can of beer and drank it down in a few thirsty gulps. "Aren't we supposed to do this before?" he said, licking the foam from his upper lip.

I did not even pretend to know what he was talking about. I sat up, the sheet pulled up to my neck like a shroud. "Do what?"

"Imbibe."

"Imbibe? Imbibe before what?"

David reached over for another can. He'd begun dressing again, his spent energy sealed inside his clothes like a package labeled "return to sender." "You know, to get in the mood."

The remote control to the VCR was next to me. While David and I had been performing our own little drama on my futon, I'd managed to turn off the movie and take control of the scene, consciously trying not to pay homage in any way to the actress who had so quickly worn down David's resistance. Now I was in need of a new role to play, anything that did not require me to continue this conversation. "Do you want to finish the movie?" I asked.

We finished the movie. Relaxed, David lay back and absorbed the flashes of light from the screen like a sunbather on the beach. In looking at him it was hard to tell whether he was awake or asleep or even alive at all, his body inert as though under glass, a specimen for observation. At that moment I did not especially want to study him, or the movie, or my own person, which was in danger of falling into a similar state unless I took the right steps. I stood up and stretched and said good night. The movie was still running, and David was asleep now for sure; I could see it in the drool at the corner of his mouth. I took the remaining cans of beer and ran a bath.

The next morning, while we were still asleep, the phone rang. Reflexively David reached over and picked up the receiver, his hello rising from a place in his throat that was not yet ready to greet the day. There was a pause, then some more words, and by the time I had opened my eyes and determined that the stranger lying next to me was still a stranger, David was fully engaged in conversation, the phone pressed firmly against his ear.

"The position of the planets on my forehead?" I heard him say. Then he leaped out of bed and headed for the closet mirror. "Hold on, let me check."

Abby is a woman, and I am a woman. When we are hungry, we both eat. But according to a simple law of physics, if we were to lie on our backs in a lake and slowly empty our lungs, she would float easily, while I would sink.

As he spoke, David looked out the window. The sun was shining through the trees, targeting his face like a spotlight and revealing a brightness in his eyes not caused by the glare. I started to retreat, then changed my mind and stepped forward to wrest the phone from David's hands. "I assume it's for me?"

Abby was in a good mood. "Did you get my present?" she asked without skipping a beat.

Abby loved to send packages, especially ones containing skin-care products—creams and conditioners, soaps from Scandinavia, once even a vanilla-scented lip balm formulated expressly for babies. Usually when a package arrived it meant that another of her diets had failed and she was seeking a new path. And more often than not, at the end of the path there'd be a man waiting for her.

"Enjoy the bumblebee essence!" she had written on the back of this box. "It's tons better than the jaguar drops. Those were worth shit." Inside, nestled under a bed of Styrofoam, was a small vial labeled with a picture of an oversize bumblebee charging through a field of flowers. "For claiming one's power as a strong and fully capable person," it said on the back label. "Nurtures strength, a feeling of invincibility, and supreme confidence in one's abilities."

"Yes, I got it," I said. "I meant to thank you for it sooner. What's new?"

"What's new? I'm seeing a cop," Abby said matter-of-factly. "A pig. But I checked, and there's no pig essence. Nothing that even comes close. So I got him the seagull one instead, for joy on the beach. You should see the new bikini I bought."

Instinctively I closed my eyes. "What happened to the Moroccan?"

"Oh, he's history. He always showed up in the middle of the night, when it was too late to do anything but screw. Then he just stopped coming, and never called. I think we were having too much fun."

I turned to David. He was putting his shoes on. I

held my hand over the receiver and rasped, "Are you leaving, or going out to buy bagels?"

"Ask me about the cop," Abby continued.

I sighed. "How'd you meet the cop?"

"Through an ad he put in the paper. Don't ask me what it said. Without the bumblebee essence in my system, I never would have had the guts to respond. That's why I'm calling, to see if you've tried it yet."

David walked over to me and handed me a note. It said, "I usually don't eat breakfast."

I told Abby I'd call her back and hung up the phone. David was standing by the door, fingering a sun hat hanging on the coatrack that suddenly made me feel like buying a bikini and going to the beach. "David, before you leave, I'd like to tell you something," I said, handing the note back. His shoes were still untied.

"What?"

"I usually do eat breakfast."

As though looking for evidence, he glanced in the direction of the kitchen. "Oh, sorry, I guess that didn't occur to me."

I bent down to help him tie his shoes. "It's just one of those things," I said, making a double knot.

*

David and I went on a double date with Prema and her boyfriend, Raj. I met Prema and Raj at Maharajah and we took a table for four that put us within arm's length of a statue of Kama, the Indian love god who was burned to ashes after trying to rouse the passion of the greater god Shiva. David arrived half an hour late, a little out of breath and disoriented, just as our appetizers were being cleared. Instead of apologizing, he pointed to the one remaining chutney-smeared plate on the table and said, "Is that for me?"

During the main course Raj asked David and me how we met, offering his and Prema's story first. "I was shopping for spices in the back of an Indian grocery store that also sold clothing. The door of a broom closet opened and Prema came out in a purple-and-green sari, looking for a mirror. When the owner of the store saw me staring, he took me by the arm and stood me directly in front of Prema. 'Here is your mirror,' he told her, lifting my shoulders to make me stand straighter. 'Look in it carefully, and it will tell you everything you need to know.'"

Prema turned to Raj and lifted a piece of naan from his plate. "You are such a romantic," she teased. "But that really is how it happened, I can't deny it."

I looked at David and waited for him to tell, with equal poignancy, the story of our first encounter. But at that moment his energy was being channeled elsewhere, to the fork in his hand, mining through the heap of food on his plate as if in search of the appetizers he had missed but not forgotten about.

"We met at the office, at my desk," I said, handing David a napkin. "David was taking a coffee break and didn't know where to set his cup down."

It was still early. The restaurant was just starting to fill up, with young couples mostly, a few of the women in saris. Sitting next to David was not easy;

whenever his eyes were on me I could receive them only sidelong, like a driver checking his rearview mirror. When our elbows touched, it was as extensions of the utensils in our hands, crossing over to the border between our plates for an errant pea or patch of rice. I thought of the bumblebee potion that Abby had sent and the accompanying brochure advertising a new hawk essence: "For seeing and knowing precisely where one is, and where one is going." According to the brochure, it was the hardest essence to capture in a bottle.

While food was still in front of us, the waiter appeared with the check. Our table was reserved for another party at eight o'clock. After we paid, we walked together to Raj's car, David and Prema in front, Raj and I in back. While Raj and I chatted, David dove into conversation with Prema. "They'll firm right up if you soak them in salty water," I heard him say, forming with his hands the shape of some indistinct vegetable from his childhood. At a blinking "DON'T WALK" light, he grabbed Prema's hand and ran across the street. "Should we go?" Raj asked me, stepping off the curb, ready to follow. I shook my head. When we joined our dates on the other side, Prema and I traded places and we continued on as the couples we were meant to be. At Raj's car, David opened the passenger's side and helped Prema in.

"She's beautiful, isn't she?" I said as we watched them speed away. For a brief moment the street appeared empty; the traffic was still flowing but not as fast, the glow of headlights barely enough to illuminate our faces.

"Oh, I don't know," David replied, leading me to the nearest Starbucks. "There's not a woman in the world who doesn't look good in a sari."

*

The weather changed, and people's moods with it. On the bus, passengers sat sealed in their raincoats and I absorbed their collective gloominess; every morning my cubicle felt a little more cramped, the walls a little less flexible. When David stopped by to say hello my hands stayed at my computer, palpating the keys like skin. If they had reached out to touch him, he might have mistaken them for a cold wind brushing against his shoulder and returned to his desk to fetch a sweater; but they didn't reach out, even when he extended his own hands cupped around a mug of coffee. "Thanks," I said, shaking my head politely. "I'm good."

During the coffee break people were milling about the office, some completing tasks assigned to them, others creating smaller, more personal ones of their own. I saw Nicole sidling up to Steve; I saw Steve ingratiating himself with Jocelyn; I saw a woman who, for the first full month after my introduction to her, I'd habitually called "Debbie" when she wanted to be called "Deborah," and who now went exclusively by "Deb."

"Do you want me to stop by later?" David asked, taking a tentative sip from his mug.

"At my desk, you mean?"

"No, at your place. We could watch a movie."

"A movie?" I fixed my eyes on my screen saver, a

school of mottled fish darting back and forth in search of a way out. "I don't know. I'll call you."

I did not call David. Instead I called Abby, two weeks later. I was at the grocery store stocking up on chicken soup for a cold that would not go away. A woman brushed by me, her basket empty, receiving instructions by phone on what to get for dinner. "How many?" I heard her say, as she bent down to remove a pebble from her running shoe. "Why do you want so many? Don't you like the ones I make from scratch?" At one of the endless rows of cans I took out my cell phone and dialed. Abby answered, and I got right to the point. "Anyone interesting in your life these days?"

"Me," she replied, without having to think. "I'm having the time of my life."

I took down three cans, then four, then six, and dropped them in my cart. "What happened to the cop?"

"The cop? You won't believe this, but he took me to Shakespeare in the Park, and from the first act Hamlet couldn't keep his eyes off me. I should have been the one holding up his cue cards, he forgot so many lines. Paul didn't notice any of it; he was too busy nodding off. During intermission I wrote a note to Hamlet with my name and number and left it with the usher to give to him after the performance. He was so sexy in his costume—his boots went all the way up to his knees."

"Did he call you?"

"Never, the asshole. And neither did Paul. I left him a note too, at the station."

At the checkout counter I placed my items on the belt and watched the cashier scan them: "soup soup

soup soup soup soup." When he got to a head of lettuce I had tossed in as an afterthought, he put it on the scale and looked at me. "Why, that's the biggest rutabaga I've ever seen!" he exclaimed, ringing it up as lettuce. I looked down at my breasts. They did not resemble rutabagas.

"Abby, I'll call you back later," I said, suddenly vexed by everyone who was not me. On the bus I called and told her what had happened, my nose running out of control now, my tissues all used up. "Do you think it was a lewd comment, or simple vegetable humor?"

"There is nothing a man can say that is not lewd," Abby insisted, snickering into the phone. "I've never even heard of a rutabaga."

The lettuce stayed in my refrigerator for two weeks. I waited for it to wilt so I could throw it away; I waited for it to alter its form so that it would not remind me of the cashier and his comment, or of David and his gardening. On my refrigerator was a picture of David and Raj taken by Prema during our double date at Maharajah: two smiling men clinking glasses in silent celebration of the evening, and at the margin my elbow, bearing witness. I left the lettuce where it was, and took the picture down. David was handsome, I could not deny that; he was the kind of man who would wake up in the morning to examine his chin in the mirror and end up lingering over the rest of his face. He was also the kind of man who would stand next to his girlfriend while she kicked a magical Indian tree, and then turn around just as it burst into bloom.

I put the picture in an envelope and sealed it.

Abby called a week later, out of breath, as though just returning from an early-morning run. "Thanks for the picture," she said in a rush of air. "What am I supposed to do with it?"

It was a legitimate question. "The picture is of David," I explained. "He's yours if you want him. I'll just give him your number and he'll call. I'm sure of it."

"Which one is David?"

I had to think for a minute, conjure up his image one last time. "The one on the left, with the blue eyes."

Abby hesitated. "On the left? What about the one on the right?"

"Raj?"

"I'll take him instead."

I imagined Prema in her sari, a woman as beautiful as her man was handsome. "Raj is not available," I said sternly. "What's wrong with David?"

"Nothing, really. But look at his teeth," Abby said. "Do you see how they protrude, and how the corner of his mouth folds? That's bad news. And it doesn't stop there. I found a wrinkle on his forehead that crosses his line of Mars. On account of that one little wrinkle—and you can only see it if you hold it up to the light—David has a good chance of meeting a violent death, and may even end up as a beggar. I would give him a chance, I really would," she said, slowing down, "but not every man is for me. In fact, I'm seeing someone now who I'm beginning to have doubts about—Charlie. I met him at a kite-flying contest. On the surface he's as sweet as a lamb, but the first time we went to bed and I called him Chuck, it sent him into a rage and made him flaccid immediately."

I wanted to hang up the phone but instead held it closer to my ear and walked over to the balcony, letting Abby's words pass through me and into the open air. Stepping out, I took in the scents around me, spring flowers and the exhaust of a high-powered lawn mower three flights below. I thought of David as a boy in his mother's garden and then as a man talking to Abby on the phone, the two of them like companion plants, one diminishing the other's natural repelling ability as they grew together. I recalled the way David had touched me in bed, his hands clambering over me like a vine, his nail-bitten fingers not the tingling brambles I wanted them to be.

"Hey! Are you still there?" Abby called into the receiver.

I peered over the railing. The lawn was almost even now, manicured like a woman's fingers, groomed like a man's shaven face. I held the phone to my heart and watched the mower's blade pass over a final patch of grass until it merged with the soil beneath it, swiftly and without effort, in silent acceptance at being part of the land.

Bargabourg Remembers

Professor Bargabourg had never been grabbed before, either by a stranger or by a friend. Although this time it was a stranger hanging on to the nape of his neck outside a cigar store on Fifty-Seventh Street—though like a friend, Professor Bargabourg could not help but observe, the man hung on like a friend—he hoped that the next time it would be a friend indeed, and preferably, if he had any say in the matter, a woman.

A knife held this close to a man's skin, Professor Bargabourg observed further—disappointed that the blade did not shine under the street lamp, that his attacker did not at least cast a shadow—loses the power to leave even a trace of lasting evidence on the consciousness. The moment it is withdrawn and repocketed, he thought, if I am still alive, I will have forgotten everything. This fear—and he was terribly afraid—will have made me forget everything. Never again will I be able to call to mind the sharpness of the blade, the force of my assailant's grip, the pulse of my jugular beneath it; the hot air, the cigars in the window, the window, the store, the street . . .

What had come to pass. Professor Bargabourg did not wish to forget it. In fact, nothing frightened him more. Believing that such experiences could be understood only by one's reeling back in all the horrible memories one's mind has tried to cast out, he forced himself to pay attention to the crime that was being committed against him. Once he had reclaimed all the data, he could process it to make it yield more than it had ever intended to give; and he might finally be able to discover why, for instance, if morality is a decision of the will, there are not as many conflicting moralities as there are wills; and why, when we need proof of our own greatness, it is not enough simply to stop someone in the street and say to him, "Look at me: I have tapped you on the shoulder, and you have stopped."

This is some of what Professor Bargabourg was thinking as he was stripped of all his possessions and knocked to the ground. Not wanting to forfeit the memory of the experience for the experience itself, he was determined to remember every detail of it, every fact and every feeling, and to commit it all to writing the moment he got home.

This is some of what he hoped to record:

From the back he approached: the back! First the hand at my neck, all five fingers, the thumbnail in need of filing. The face then, twisting around like a jack-in-the-box to meet my own: white, not black; eyes deep in discussion. In lieu of a command, a knife at my Adam's apple, holding it in place. (How I ached to swallow!)

A drunk walked toward us and disappeared into an alley, presumably to relieve himself (to relieve himself of me?). I dropped my briefcase onto my foot. My assailant impatiently kicked it into the street. When I saw that he did not value what was inside, I valued it twofold.

Lecture notes. A French-English dictionary. Three ball-point pens.

My attacker's hands did not tremble. This disappointed me. Instinctively, I held my arms above my head; just as instinctively, he forced them down. When I tried to stand up straight, he pushed me against the shop window. When I told him that my wallet was in my right pocket, he reached for the left one.

He pulled the wallet from my pocket, and I remembered Angelika. At home, poring over the wallet's contents, he would find Angelika's picture and stop to catch his breath. Angelika, rushing at him with her icy eyes, blouse half buttoned, raven hair tied like a tourniquet around the top of her head. Would he not reach out for Angelika then, try to lift her from the picture and onto his lap? Would he not recall the heat below my hairline, and try to transfer it to the woman who had thrown herself out of my house the same way he had thrown me to the ground?

The violation of a mugging, of his hand at my neck, his dagger at my throat! I was neither a friend nor an enemy to him. It was all for Angelika!

*

The moment he entered his apartment, Professor Bargabourg threw open his briefcase to retrieve a pen, but it was too late. His mind failed to recall even a sense of the account he had mentally written in the street. Indistinct images were all he could conjure up: street, man, knife, wallet, alley. Above all, alley. Why?

When he tried to think in feelings, none came to him. He closed his eyes for a sign and saw darkness. Was that the sign? He opened his eyes and saw light. Was that the sign? He took the cap off the pen and wrote in his notebook, "History is a chronicle of the crimes of humanity (darkness), and of man's struggle against them (light)."

He walked over to the window and looked out. Here is what he did not see:

A startled face staring back at him; an empty can rolling toward the tire of a parked car; a parked car; a passing car; four members of the same family holding hands before charging down the street; a street; a taxi driver rolling down the window of his cab and blowing his nose into a handkerchief.

Professor Bargabourg felt for the wallet in his pocket. It was not there. What had been in it? Money, ten, twenty dollars at most. Credit cards. A folded-up sheet of stamps. In vain, he tried to recall what he had been thinking about the moment he was attacked, or what he had been thinking about the moment before he was attacked. Was it his lecture course at the university? His plans to travel abroad for the summer? The fullness of his aging bladder?

As his mind offered nothing more, he thought it might be best to consult a doctor, who, as an agent of recovery, could try to help him piece together the lost details of the assault. But what kind of doctor? A brain specialist? A psychiatrist? A cardiologist? Or perhaps a spiritual doctor—a priest? A minister? A rabbi? What could any of these people tell him that would put him on the road to remembering? That the mugger, in robbing a man of his knowledge, proved, once and for all, that honesty and decency are the standard of fools?

Professor Bargabourg sat in his kitchen, fingering a butter knife. Once, in the midst of a heated argument, Angelika had lunged at him with such a knife, perhaps this very knife, stopping several inches from his heart, not close enough even to graze his sweater. Only then did he see the seriousness of the argument. While the knife was still in its drawer, he had not been aware that they were fighting at all.

And when they separated, it did not feel like a separation. He wrote letters to Angelika every day, entreating her to come to her senses and return to where she belonged, with him, in his house. Out of his own hunger, he clawed at her absence and brought her into being. When the telephone rang, he spilled out the entirety of his feelings for her before even picking up the receiver. He did not know that the moment she stepped out the door, she would not leave anything of herself behind. In every corner he sensed that she was still there, like a shadow trying to reshape itself into a streak of blinding light. He did not know that when he let her act of her own free will, his own will would be obliterated, snuffed out like the fire that had stopped burning in her heart.

Professor Bargabourg dropped the knife into his breast pocket and went out for a walk.

It was dark now. The sounds in the street were different from before, less sure of themselves, while the people passing by walked with quick, confident steps, determined to get where they were going. Professor Bargabourg was an exception; he did not have a destination in mind. He knew only that he wanted to be outside, hoping the fresh air might reconnect the faulty wiring inside his head. Once healed, he would be able to reclaim the city as his own and not feel uneasy about walking at night without a wallet in his pocket. Then, if he was mugged a second time, he'd be able to write about it.

Feeling hungry, he stopped and bought a soft pretzel with a crumpled dollar from his front pocket. Before taking a bite, he tried to prepare himself for the possibility that he would no longer be able to recognize the flavor of a pretzel, that the attack had impaired not only his memory, but the ability of his brain to receive messages from the taste receptors on his tongue as well. He looked at the pretzel in his hand and saw that it was a pretzel. He held it up to his nose and smelled that it was a pretzel. On the vendor's cart stood a large squirt bottle of mustard. Professor Bargabourg had never cared for mustard, but he felt he had no choice. He squirted a liberal yellow snake of sauce onto his pretzel and took a bite. The sharpness went right to his head.

When he approached the cigar store on Fifty-Seventh Street, he instinctively reached for the wallet that was no longer in his pocket. He sat down on the curb and watched the traffic crawl by. He leaned against a lamppost and let the glow of the light warm his head. For half an hour he waited without expectation, marveling at a mother and baby who passed by without incident; at an old woman in a fur coat, her chin tilted skyward; at a businessman carrying a briefcase nearly identical to Professor Bargabourg's own. Everyone in the right place at the right time. When a young woman tripped on a crack in the sidewalk, Professor Bargabourg experienced a moment of gratitude, and graciously helped her to her feet again.

It was a feeling that shamed him. Before Angelika's abrupt departure, he had always wished others well. If a colleague published a book or received a grant, Professor Bargabourg was happy for him. If a student sent a postcard from some tropical island during the semester break, Professor Bargabourg saved the stamp and put it in an album. This generosity of spirit had served him well over the years, helping to secure invitations to dinner parties, offers to travel abroad, even discounts from some of the most stubborn antiquarians. The first shadow fell when Angelika picked up one of his favorite books and suggested they read it together. Hungrily they devoured the pages, taking turns reading aloud like animals sharing a kill. But when they stopped to discuss the first chapter, it became clear that they were driven by contrary passions. Where he had always read hope, she read despair; where he found a deepening of wisdom in a character's vantage, she saw a lapse of moral judgment in his actions. These differences of interpretation were not superficial; they rocked the very foundation of their relationship. Suddenly he was forced to question all the assumptions he had ever made about himself and the people around him. And when he tried to embrace Angelika at the end of the evening, she accused him of looking her in the eye only to see the reflection of his own face.

Testing his fingers for flexibility as he walked, he

imagined them sinking into someone's neck. Professor Bargabourg had never grabbed anyone before. Would he sneak up from the rear, like a shadow, or strike head-on, unafraid to show his formidable face? Would he bark orders at his victim, or employ a silent blow to the belly? And when it was all over—when his fingers were once again part of his hands—would an apology be in order? If so, who should apologize to whom? The assailant to the victim, for disturbing his equilibrium, or the victim to the assailant, for disturbing his?

But he was in no mood to apologize. He was interested in only one thing—recouping his losses, restoring his memory to its rightful owner. If he could be in possession of himself again, there would be no need for apologies; he could forgive anyone anything. In the past, this would not have been the case. In the past, when a wrong had been committed against him, he would seek out the agent of the injustice and force her to refashion it into something benign. Thus a lashing out could evolve into lovemaking, a bitter accusation into renewed vows of fidelity. Whatever the injury, Professor Bargabourg never had to compromise himself to heal it.

But tonight the pain lingered. Should he stop someone and ask for a remedy? Should he knock someone to the ground and demand one? His condition, after all, was serious, and called for serious actions. A man who relies on his mind for his daily bread and finds only a few crumbs in his pocket at the end of the day is no longer a man. Today he could not remember the details of the mugging. And tomorrow? What would he not remember then? That even in the years of plenty, he could not hold on to what he had?

Professor Bargabourg had never grabbed anyone before. Stopping in front of a building far enough from his own to feel he was owed some reward for the distance traveled, he reached confidently for the knife in his pocket. When Angelika walked out of the building, a stack of gray stanching the blackness in her hair, he was poised.

Naftali

I would like to believe in the possibility that putting words on paper can make them true, that when Naftali sat across from me on the hard edge of a couch whose plump cushions could have kept him all afternoon, he saw in my face a clock counting down the seconds to his departure, and bolted before he could blush. I have seen this happen before, men who confront their desires by covering them up and running away. And I knew that Naftali often ran away, sometimes for a week and sometimes for a year, looking for experiences that were compatible with the rovings of his mind. I imagined the passions that inspired his odysseys took hold of him long before we met, perhaps from the day he was born, three days before the outbreak of the Six-Day War, on the freshly overturned earth of a vineyard in Petah Tikvah. In the end it was always I who blushed, stammering out my broken Hebrew like a sick horse, wondering if this time he would stay long enough for the teakettle to boil.

It was easy for me to love him without knowing him. He lived in Jerusalem, a city that belonged to my heart like no other. But that was not all. He was always changing his destiny, subverting it to make it serve him better. He would return to old places before moving to new ones. He would tell stories about his grandfather in the first person. When he spoke, he would fix his voice so that it would not rise above a whisper, and women would lean closer to listen—that is, I would lean closer to listen, and whatever it was that I heard, it was never enough. It was always just the beginning. The rest I had to take on faith. I was constantly creating Naftali anew.

Once he invited me over for dinner. To settle my nerves I spent the whole day shopping for a gift. I went to Steimatzky and scoured the place for a book I thought he might not already own. Naftali's apartment was crammed with books—I knew this without ever having seen it. At the moshav where his parents still lived, which I *had* visited, the entire toolshed was given over to his collection. Next to an old plow, on a shelf, stood a first edition of Elie Wiesel's *Night* in Yiddish. I had not known this book was originally written in Yiddish; Naftali told me. The information had flowed from his blue eyes like an embrace.

Needless to say, it was not a sit-down dinner. It was not really a dinner at all. Naftali sat in the kitchen, chopping cucumbers and tomatoes. I watched him, standing up. His hands were pale and smooth, not a rough spot on them. Diaspora hands. The tips of his fingers were unusually flat: the result, perhaps, of having spent too much time pressed against Naftali's temples. While I observed these details my horse's mouth galloped forward, slowing down only to correct a mispronounced word or ask to be reminded of a forgotten one. The more clumsy my Hebrew became, the faster I charged. I spoke about everything and nothing—the long lines at the post office, the reign of King David, Central Park, walking the ramparts of the Old City.

With every attempt to create harmony out of Naftali's chaos, I created only more chaos. I could have given up then, admitted to myself that while we might have shared the same roots, there was no point in carrying on like an archaeologist, trying to produce evidence of an unbroken past. But at that moment Naftali pointed to the living room window that overlooked the Israel Museum and said, "Do you know why the Shrine of the Book is shaped like a womb? To represent our national will to survive."

There was bread to go with the salad, and hummus. I studied the cucumber and tomato on my plate like a puzzle, trying to find in each piece a part of Naftali I could understand. Had we been speaking English, I would have asked him more about our national will to survive, and about the oleander tree growing outside his window. Cannily I would have linked his fingers to the food in my mouth and searched his eyes for the kibbutz from which they came.

"Hm," I replied. "And to see it from your window."

I got up to fetch the book I had brought him, a Hebrew translation of some Philip Roth novel I had never read. I don't remember which one it was because it was such an unsatisfying gesture, giving Naftali someone else's words instead of my own. When I handed it to him he looked uncomfortable, as though this physical act of transfer required more of a commitment than he was willing to make. After removing the tissue paper he whispered, "Thank you, but you shouldn't have gone to the trouble. I'll return it as soon as I'm through."

"But it's yours to keep," I insisted. "It's nothing, really."

"Well, we'll see. *Todah rabah.*"

The telephone rang and Naftali went into his bedroom to answer it, halfway closing the door behind him. Through the gap I could see him stretched out on his bed, speaking quietly into the receiver, and for a moment the temptation of flight was so strong I had to hold on to the edge of the table to resist it.

Naftali returned to me a few minutes later, a warm glow on his face. "Would you like to go for a walk?" he asked, already reaching for his jacket. Our dinner sat on the table, half eaten, the water glasses empty from having never been filled.

I did not want to go for a walk. I did not want to follow Naftali as he headed, impervious to the intimacy that emanated from the Jerusalem air, straight up the alley that led to my apartment building. For this was what he'd meant when he made his suggestion: that the evening was over and it was time for me to go home. To protect himself from any unwanted entanglement he would walk with his hands in his pockets and his head down; if any human closeness threatened to evolve along the way, he would shake it off by asking after my family back in America, my mother, father, two brothers, and pet dog.

We were separated by only an alley, but we were not neighbors. Our streets, named after rabbis of competing dynasties, ran parallel to each other and, as such, would never meet. The alley had steps, which Naftali took two at a time. I kept his pace and tried to catch the excess breath he exhaled from his effort. "How is your family?" I asked him preemptively as we neared the top.

We were in the street again before he answered. "Thank God, everyone is fine." *B'seder gamur.* Very fine.

The sound of a piano emerged from an apartment window as we passed, and Naftali and I turned our heads toward the music at the same time. "I can hear this woman from my living room every night," he said, stopping for a moment to listen. "She knows Schubert very well."

The music flowed with an energy I did not welcome. If the window above us had been closed we still would have been able to hear the sound, but it would have reached us like a whisper, a warm breath in our ears, and Naftali might have seen me the rest of the way home. I smiled weakly. "And I can hear her from my bedroom."

He left for America the following week, to study Yiddish. That's how he was; it did not even seem strange to me. During his absence, I pursued my studies at the university with unusual vigor. In a single day I read Herzl's *Altneuland* and signed up to tutor a blind Arab in conversational English. Another day, I listened in terror during Yehuda Bauer's course on the Holocaust, which Naftali had taken a few semesters earlier, then hurried to the cafeteria for a bowl of matzo-ball soup. I was on my way to the library afterward when I saw Miriam walking toward me through the turnstile, her false teeth smiling at me in two perfectly straight rows.

At the sight of her, my plans for the rest of the day disintegrated. Gently I took her by the elbow. "Shalom, Miriam!" I shouted, to make sure she heard. "Are you on your way home?"

Miriam was on her way home, and I went with her.

The bus ride could not have been slower, taking us through French Hill and the narrow streets of Mea She'arim like a tour guide with a long itinerary. On a normal day there would have been lots to see, not thick forests of spruce or deep wadis obscured by dust clouds, but laundry flapping from clotheslines, black-bordered death notices tacked to billboards, and rows of public housing units testifying to the Jews' return to Jerusalem. But I was too impatient to focus on anything beyond where we were going, to the library in Miriam's living room, from which Naftali had acquired several of the rarest books in his collection.

As she usually did, Miriam led me to the couch and opened up a photo album. Many of the faces were young, and did not get older as the pages piled up.

"This is Lili, in Frankfurt," Miriam said, pointing to a young girl with pigtails on the very last page. "We used to tell people we were twins."

I stared hard at the picture, then tried to shake my head free of the image. "Do you have any photos from when you served in the Palmach?" I asked.

She closed the album. "Somewhere there is one, of me on a horse belonging to the British high commissioner. I remember this man well. He took a liking to me, but not to what I was fighting for. When he came to Palestine to visit with a delegation of Zionists, he told them he didn't think the Jews would survive much longer. He told them this and still they offered him sugar with his tea."

I let my eyes wander over to the bookshelves, looking for a gap that Naftali's hands might have made. To my disappointment, I found many gaps, made by many hands, and a stepladder in the corner that Miriam's late husband had used whenever he needed a quote from Heine. "Where have all the books gone?" I asked.

"*Ach,* the books. To whoever wants them, mostly dealers, some *Liebhaber.* It was Weli's wish," she replied. "My eyes were only good when he was alive."

"Can I ask in which category you would place Naftali?"

"Naftali?"

"Naftali." I couldn't say his name often enough.

"In the category of *Liebhaber,* of course," Miriam said, squeezing my arm. "The passion in that man could fill the national archives at Givat Ram."

*

My mother called and asked if I was seeing anyone. "Don't be shy about it," she insisted, suspecting something. "I was shy with my own mother and we didn't talk for twenty years. Come on, who's the lucky man?"

I wanted to tell my mother everything, but there was nothing to tell. "His name is Naftali," I said. "Like the tribe."

"The tribe?" said my mother. "Where are you, in Africa? Tell me what he does, how he treats you. Is he in debt like all Israelis?"

I thought of Miriam and said, "He's got lots of interests, lots of passions. He collects books; he likes languages. But he always seems a little melancholy." I paused, expecting my mother to interrupt. And she did.

"He sounds like a luftmensch," she said. "A Jew with

his head in the clouds. Just like your father, when I first met him."

"Oh, he's not like Dad at all," I assured her, picturing my father standing under the bright lights of his operating room, ready to cut open a patient's heart. "He's much more subtle."

*

When Naftali returned from America, he did not call me. I discovered his return by accident, outside a fruit-and-vegetable stand in the center of town. There he was, filling a bag with apricots and squinting in the sun, while I stood one stall over, rifling through a crate of tomatoes. I stood silently, waiting for him to see me, knowing that it could not work any other way, that he would have to see me first if I was to exist at all, never mind that I existed only for him. The tomato man lifted my bag onto the scale, then tossed it back to me. "Four shekels," he said.

As I was paying, I heard his voice. "In Israel, shopping outdoors is one of life's greatest pleasures. Shalom, Dina."

I looked up with my heart spinning in my head. "Shalom, Naftali," I said, with a rush of air. "*Vos macht a Yid?*"

It was the only Yiddish greeting I knew. Naftali acknowledged it with a soft smile and together we walked down the aisles of Machane Yehuda, the tents flapping above us like a wedding canopy. In front of a row of fish heads Naftali reached into his bag and pulled out an apricot, then turned to me and asked, "And how is your family?"

The question endeared him to me as much as it made me want to cry. "*B'seder gamur,*" I said.

"I have forgotten what state they live in—Iowa?"

"Ohio."

Silently I watched him rub the apricot against his shirt. It was hypnotic, like watching a pendulum swing; there was no urgency in the action, no tension of ambush. Everything about Naftali bespoke a calmness that I could describe only as anachronistic. Nobody in Israel was calm, and if there was ever an age when Jews had dared to be so, it was certainly not now. For a moment I thought the apricot might pass from his hand to mine, a gesture that would have sustained me for years. But a second later it went into his mouth and disappeared down his throat. At some point the pit must have emerged, but not while I was looking.

We walked farther. An old beggar came up to us shaking a tin can, and Naftali dropped a shekel into it. "*Sh'tihiye bari,*" he said, wishing the man good health.

"How was New York?" I asked.

Naftali considered the question, still focusing on the beggar nearby, then turned his blue eyes directly toward me to answer it. "The Yiddish at YIVO is not the Yiddish I know from Lvov."

"You know Yiddish from Lvov?"

"My grandfather was born there."

"Oh, I see."

But I still could not make myself seen by Naftali, and at these words I lost him. We walked a few more meters, side-by-side but not together. At the end of the market a bus pulled up and Naftali stepped onto it. "Are you going home?" he asked.

It was his way of saying good-bye. "I've got some more shopping to do," I said, getting ready to watch him disappear again. "But let's get together soon."

"*A zay gezunt,*" said Naftali, and he was gone.

*

A man who was not Naftali called me on the telephone and invited me for a drink. I put on a skirt and walked down the street to the Laromme Hotel, passing on my way a fleet of town cars spiriting the prime minister off to an equally important engagement. Assaf was waiting for me in the lobby, radiating good health and stability, a full head of curls framing his tanned face.

We sat at a table in the hotel café and stared hard at each other. Assaf asked me questions, and I answered them.

"Do you have a boyfriend?"

"No."

"Do you work?"

"No."

"Did your parents buy you an apartment?"

"No."

Then it was my turn. "How do you know Miriam?" I asked.

"Miriam, the *yekke*? I'm her accountant. Without those checks from Germany every month, she'd be in overdraft up to her knees." Assaf stared at me even harder, seeking favor. His eyes, like his hair, were a healthy brown, big and benevolent and nearly obscured by his lashes, which hung over them like palm fronds in the desert.

"Germany is waiting for her to die so they can stop sending them," I said.

"May she live to one hundred and twenty," Assaf replied.

I liked Assaf, and he liked me. In a single weekend we traveled all of Israel together, renting snorkeling gear in Eilat one day and picking wildflowers in the Golan Heights the next. The farther we drove from Jerusalem, the freer I felt; the weight of that walled city fell from my shoulders like pomegranates from a tree. By the time we had reached our halfway point at Netanya, I was giddy with wanderlust. Assaf saw the eagerness in my face and took credit for its being there. At every falafel stand we stopped to snap photos.

Along a coastal road past Ashkelon we pulled over at an old water tower lying on its side, riddled by artillery shells. Around it were flowering trees and a little pond, and benches for contemplating the ruins. Assaf and I sat down on one of these benches and threw pebbles at the rusty steel beams in front of us. "What war do you think this is from?" I asked, tilting my face toward the sun.

"Forty-eight, for sure," Assaf replied. "We're only a few hundred yards from the old border with Egypt."

I looked all around me, half expecting the pyramids to appear over the horizon. Instead my eyes landed on a giant bronze man looming over a sycamore tree, his right hand clutching a grenade. I nudged Assaf and pointed to the statue. "Who's that?"

For Assaf, the spot where we were sitting was not new. He had seen the water tower before, and the trees and pond and benches. On a high school field trip he had leaned against the feet of the bronze man and cracked sunflower seeds, and with his army platoon had camped out in the citrus grove of a nearby kibbutz bearing the man's name.

"That's Mordechai Anielewicz," Assaf explained. "He was the commander of the Warsaw Ghetto uprising, just out of high school." He stood up from the bench and cocked his head in the opposite direction. "*Yalla.* Let's go get some lunch."

We drove to a fish restaurant in Ashkelon and took a table overlooking the sea. In the sand below, beach umbrellas obscured the bodies of sunbathers and children played tirelessly in the water, screaming at the tops of their lungs. Turning my attention inland, I watched Assaf tear off pieces of his napkin and release them over the rail. His fingers worked rapidly, like the legs of an industrious spider. When they slowed down again he turned to me and shrugged his shoulders. "It never snows in this country," he said. "There aren't enough napkins."

The return trip to Jerusalem felt like a funeral procession. It was slow, labored, onerous. Assaf's car could barely make it up the hill leading into the city, and the dryness of the air forced me to summon up all the things I had to feel sad about. As we approached the central bus station, a number 9 Egged bus pulled out in front of us and we followed it all the way to Machane Yehuda, where it stopped to let off a handful of shoppers armed with collapsible carts.

Still, knowing this would be the last time Assaf drove me home, I did not mind the eternity it took. At each red light I tried to make my intentions known. I told him it was time to return to my studies, and that I had an entire semester's worth of course work to catch up on. I told him that I had applied for a job sorting books at the library, and that I had signed up for an intensive, three-hour-a-day *ulpan* to improve my Hebrew. I told him these and other things, but what I could not tell him was the most convincing thing of all: that I could not see him again because I belonged to someone else. Or rather: because someone else belonged to me. But that was not right either; what I could not tell him was something I was only just beginning to understand: that I could not see him again because Jerusalem belonged to Naftali, and no one else. That is exactly how it was.

*

One day I received a package in the mail from Naftali. Inside was a large bundle of papers, and on top a Post-it that read, "Good luck with the final exam. It's not easy."

I carried the papers to my bedroom and leafed through them. They were organized chronologically, with Roman numerals: "I: Anti-Jewish Legislation, 1933–1935"; "II: The SS"; "III: The *Einsatzgruppen*"; "IV: The Death Camps"; etc.

Naftali's notes were copious. In vain I searched the margins for doodles; my eyes raced across the pages for clues of any kind—underlined words, italics, a place where the pen had run out of ink. I found nothing, only death and destruction. The Jews of Germany, Austria, Poland; the Jews of France, Belgium, Luxembourg; the Jews of Hungary, Romania, Bulgaria, Yugoslavia. Naftali's handwriting was beautiful; his alephs looked like cats arching their backs.

I called him a week later, when I was through.

"Shalom, Naftali?" I had not heard myself say his name in close to a month. "I got your package. *Todah rabah.* It's very comprehensive."

"I hope it's all there," he said. "There was a lot of material to cover."

As we spoke I hurriedly flipped through the pages, trying to keep the conversation going at whatever cost. "In the section about Poland I couldn't find a heading for Lvov," I gambled, placing my finger between 'Łódź' and 'Petrików.' "I know that's where your grandfather came from, and I wanted to learn more about it."

A sound like the low trill of a horn emerged from Naftali's throat. "Lvov was a city of one hundred thousand Jews, a city of great culture and creativity," he said. "My grandfather had a happy life there."

"What year did he leave for Israel?"

"Leave for Israel? His heart was always in Israel. Even as a young boy. He came from a proud family of Zionists."

I did not know what else to say to Naftali. The hot winds of a *hamsin* were spreading across Jerusalem, stirring up trails of fine dust in every direction. I could smell it through the open window: it filled my mouth and forced it shut. I would have liked to think it had the same effect on Naftali, that were it not for the dust penetrating his nostrils he would have tried to embrace the necessity of human discourse and allowed himself to emerge, if only gradually, from the hiding place in which he had taken refuge for so long.

We said good-bye and I packed up the box of notes and took them to Miriam. She was sitting at the kitchen table when I walked in, peeling apples for a fruit compote. An empty Augarten serving bowl with a pink rose painted at the bottom teetered at the edge of the table. When she saw the contents of the box, she stopped what she was doing. "This he sends you, instead of flowers?" she said, wiping her hands on a dish towel. "Take it away, please. I have enough ghosts in my house already."

I cradled the box in my arms. "I think it's his way of communicating," I said unconvincingly. "I think we're beginning to understand each other."

Together we sat on the couch and looked at pictures. "This is Lili, in Frankfurt." Miriam pointed to her sister's pigtails. Then suddenly she snapped the album shut. "So what was the matter with Assaf?"

It was hard for me to make the leap from Lili's pigtails to Assaf, from violent death to snowflakes sailing over the sea. "Nothing was the matter with Assaf," I said, closing my eyes but still seeing Lili. "Maybe he was a little young for me."

Miriam clasped her hands together, perhaps to stop them from slapping me. "Young? And you like that Jerusalem has made Naftali old?"

I did, very much. "He's what I came to this country to find," I said, shrugging.

Taking the notes, I left Miriam's house and headed for Naftali's. The streets were full of people like me, carrying their burdens from one place to another, stopping once, but never more than that, to admire the bougainvillea cascading over fences and stone ledges. As I approached Ha-Rav Berlin Street, I encountered myself in every passerby: in a man walking his dog, the long leather leash wound tightly around his hand like tefillin; in two women pushing babies in strollers; in a young girl weighed down by a schoolbag, tossing an empty Coke can into the street. All these people were me, and I was them; whichever route I took to Naftali's, it would be through a terrain of total fragmentation.

Outside a newspaper stand I put down the box to scan the day's headlines and gather myself together. Before I could do either, a rough, hairy hand landed on my shoulder. "What's new in the world?"

I looked up and took shelter in the shade of Assaf's eyelashes. "Shalom, Assaf," I said. "I—"

"Never mind," said Assaf, quick to forgive. He leaned over to pick up Naftali's box. "Where are you going? I'll walk with you."

I tried to walk, but my arms would not cooperate. Instead of swinging at my sides they kept reaching out for the box in Assaf's arms, the coffin that carried Naftali. "That's OK, I can hold it," I said nonchalantly. "It's not heavy."

Assaf shifted the box into the palm of one hand and

held it out to me like a flower. "*B'vakasha,*" he said with a bow. "With pleasure."

I thanked Assaf and we walked a little farther, then said good-bye, and I was alone again, standing outside the door to Naftali's building, propped open by a small slab of Jerusalem stone. Inside, a row of six narrow mailboxes lined the wall, the first bearing the name, in small Hebrew letters, "Dr. Naftali Simon." I climbed some steps and rang the doorbell.

Naftali opened the door, and words tumbled out of my mouth. "Since when are you a PhD?" I asked, pointing in the direction of the mailboxes below. "Here, I brought your notes back. *Todah rabah* again, but I decided not to take the exam. The material is too much for me. It should be too much for anyone in this country. Wasn't it too much for you?"

He invited me in, but did not answer my questions. Instead he said, in that muted voice of his, which reached its object like a pillow, "Shalom, Dina. You are looking more Israeli each day."

A suitcase filled with books and underwear lay open on the living room floor. "I'm going on reserve duty tomorrow, please excuse the mess," Naftali said, offering me a hard wooden chair to sit on while he continued packing. "Professor Bauer will be sorry you are not taking the exam. He loses a lot of students at the end of the semester."

Naftali pulled a book from the suitcase and handed it to me. "This Philip Roth would like to see us return to Europe and save Israel from a second Holocaust. What do you think of that idea?"

I was thrilled by the *us* in Naftali's sentence. "Philip

Roth is quite a satirist," I said eagerly, handing the book back to him. "Have you ever been to Europe?"

"I've been to Poland."

"To Lvov?"

"Lvov," said Naftali.

Soon the suitcase would be packed, and it would be time for me to go. But I did not want to go. Naftali was in the kitchen now, opening and closing drawers in search of something he probably did not need. I followed him there and waited for him to turn around. When he didn't, I said to Naftali in English, "Do you think love flourishes when it is deferred?"

Naftali turned and faced me, but his love of languages went only so far. "*S'licha?*" he said, begging my pardon. In his hand he held a carrot peeler.

"I'm just wondering why you went to Lvov," I said. "Poland without Jews is a ghost town, no?"

Naftali tried to squeeze by me to return to his suitcase. "It's worse than a ghost town," he said, looking pale himself. "My grandfather doesn't even have a grave."

Now it was my turn not to understand. Again. "But I thought your grandfather left Poland. Before?"

"Not before, and not after," said Naftali. "Everything was waiting for him here—a country, an apartment, a mailbox with his name on it, his children who had been sent ahead—everything. And it's still waiting for him—*Dr. Naftali Simon*—just as it was."

He left me then and retreated into his bedroom. I wanted to be close to Naftali, as close as Naftali was to the grandfather he'd never known but whose name he would always carry, so I sat down on the floor next to his suitcase. It was a Samsonite, all black but for a bright yellow ribbon he had tied to the handle to distinguish it from all the other black Samsonites traveling through the airports and train stations of the world. Slipping my ring finger through the loop of the ribbon, I turned it every which way, vowing not to stop until it shone like gold.

Naftali emerged from the bedroom with his army uniform draped over one arm, half civilian, half soldier. "A Jew must always keep a packed bag under his bed, in the event that he has to leave in a hurry," he said, folding the uniform as though it were a pair of pajamas.

Breaking my vow, I withdrew my finger from the ribbon and rubbed away the indentation from my skin. "But you're never here," I said. "You're always somewhere else."

Naftali bent down and slipped his uniform into the suitcase, smiling as if I had just made a joke. "*Nu,* should we go for a walk?" He zipped up the suitcase and wheeled it to the door. From the back, he looked like an old man.

On HaRav Berlin Street the sun was setting, casting its dying light on the faces of Israelis heading home for the evening. Naftali led our way into the mouth of the alley and I followed, leaving the flow of traffic to continue without us. Halfway up, I bent down to remove a pebble from my sandal, and when I stood up again he was so far ahead of me it was impossible to see where he had gone. I had wanted to have one last conversation with Naftali before letting him go, one final exchange to make him see that where he came from, I came from too. But there was too great a distance between us, and it was all I could do not to turn around and wait for him on the other side of the street.

Acknowledgments

Thanks to the following publications, where these stories first appeared, sometimes in different versions: *AGNI* ("Thinking in Third Person"), *Atlantic* ("Contamination"), *Bellingham Review* ("Swan Street"), *Carve* ("Floating on Water"), *Colorado Review* ("Invasions"), *Fiction* ("A Famine in the Land"), *Jewcy* ("Naftali"), JewishFiction.net ("Amnon"), *Los Angeles Review* ("The Four Foods"), *Michigan Quarterly Review* ("The Next Vilonsky"), *Mississippi Review* ("Bargabourg Remembers"), *Moment* ("The Worlds We Think We Know," as "Infections"), *Shenandoah* ("Two Passions for Two People"), and *Zeek* ("The Other Air").

I would like to thank my parents, Alvin and Erna Rosenfeld, for forty-five years of encouragement, support, inspiration, and love.

Thank you to my children, Natan, Gidi, and Adin, for every day.

Thanks to my agent, Alexis Hurley, for her unmatched efforts and enthusiasm, and to my editor, Joey McGarvey, who understands each word and beyond.

Thank you to Adam Rovner for his altruism; Paul Thomas, Paul Haberman, Anat Helman, and Carmen Niekrasz.

Thank you to my brother Gavriel for reading early drafts of stories, and always in the middle of grading period.

And to Asher, who taught me everything.

EFRAT VITAL

DALIA ROSENFELD is a graduate of the Iowa Writers' Workshop. Her work has appeared in publications including the *Atlantic*, *AGNI*, *Michigan Quarterly Review*, *Mississippi Review*, and *Colorado Review*. She teaches creative writing at Bar Ilan University and lives with her three children in Tel Aviv.

Founded as a nonprofit organization in 1980, Milkweed Editions is an independent publisher. Our mission is to identify, nurture and publish transformative literature, and build an engaged community around it.

milkweed.org

Interior design by Mary Austin Speaker
Typeset in New Baskerville

English type founder, stonecutter, and letter designer John Baskerville (1706–1775) began his career as a headstone engraver, snuffbox japanner, and writing master before starting his printing business. The first book he printed took seven years to produce, during which time Baskerville was responsible for major innovations in press construction, ink, papermaking, and letter design. His work was admired by Pierre-Simon Fournier, Giambattista Bodoni, and Benjamin Franklin, among others, and revived in the 1920s by Bruce Rogers.